And then there were none.

"Three missing dogs and two missing cats?" Erin said as Val sat down at the table. "Do you really think there's a petnapper in Essex, Vallie?"

"Just a minute, everybody," Doc said. "Vallie, what exactly did Toby tell you?"

Between bites of her watermelon, Val repeated what Toby had said. "I don't think it's just a coincidence, Dad," she insisted. "It's not just _one_ dog, it's . . ."

"I know — three dogs and two cats."

Just then the doorbell rang. Teddy raced out of the kitchen and returned moments later with his friend Sparky and her mother. Sparky's eyes were red and swollen.

"Hey, Dad, listen to this!" Teddy said. "Go on, Sparky. Tell my dad about Charlie."

Sparky wiped her runny nose with the back of her hand, then wiped her hand on her shorts. "Charlie . . ." She gulped. "Charlie's _gone_!"

ANIMAL INN

PETNAPPED!

Virginia Vail

AN
APPLE
PAPERBACK

SCHOLASTIC INC.
New York Toronto London Auckland Sydney

For Beth, Stephanie, Joel, Erin, Melissa, Jessie,
Kristen, Janis, and all the other fans of
ANIMAL INN *who have written such*
wonderful letters to me.

ISBN 0-590-42799-7

12 11 10 9 8 7 6 5 4 3 2 1   0 1 2 3 4 5/9

Printed in the U.S.A.   11

First Scholastic printing, May 1990

Chapter
1

Early one bright August morning, Valentine Taylor was riding her horse, The Gray Ghost, down a narrow country lane. The only sounds she heard were the songs of birds greeting the day, and the muffled *clop clop* of The Ghost's hooves on the dirt road. It was as though she and the dapple-gray gelding were the only creatures awake in Essex, Pennsylvania — except the birds, of course.

"Do you think the early bird really *does* get the worm, Ghost?" Val asked the horse, stroking his satiny shoulder. The Ghost flicked his ears back and forth and nodded his head, whuffling softly as though in reply.

Val laughed. "I guess maybe you're right. It probably does. But I can't help feeling sorry for the worm!"

Just then The Ghost snatched a mouthful of the sweet dewy honeysuckle that grew on either side of the road. Val gave him a gentle slap. "Now you cut that out! You know you're not supposed to eat when you have your bridle on because it messes up your

1

bit." That reminded her of the latest joke her little brother Teddy had brought home from day camp yesterday — *"Why is a horse such an unusual animal? Because it eats best without a bit in its mouth!"*

Teddy would probably just be rolling out of bed around now, Val thought. And her eleven-year-old sister Erin would be in the kitchen of the big stone house on Old Mill Road, getting breakfast ready. Unlike Val, Erin liked to cook, and she was good at it, too. She loved fixing breakfast for the family, and usually Val loved to eat it, except on beautiful mornings like this when she just couldn't wait to bike out to her father's veterinary clinic, Animal Inn, saddle up The Ghost, and go for an early ride. Today she'd had some yogurt and an orange before she left the house. That would be enough to see her through until she met her best friend, Jill Dearborne, around noon for the picnic they'd planned on the banks of Muskrat Lake.

The Ghost ambled along the lane beneath the thick, leafy branches of the trees that formed a green arch overhead, and Val pulled in the reins, slowing him to a stop when they reached the top of a little rise. From here, she could look out over the rich, rolling Pennsylvania farmland and see the buildings that made up Animal Inn. They were so far away that they looked like toys. The Small Animal Clinic, recently expanded to include a boarding kennel, was next to the Large Animal Clinic — a big, white

2

barn — where The Ghost had his stall.

"You know, Ghost, as much as I love helping Dad at Animal Inn, it's pretty neat to have more time to spend with you," Val told her horse. "I wanted to work every single day during summer vacation, but Dad wouldn't let me. He said I ought to just hang out and enjoy the summer. That's why I'm only working three days a week. And today's one of my days off!"

The Ghost snorted and stamped, looking hopefully at more honeysuckle, but Val tightened the reins.

"No way, José!" she said. "When we get back to your pasture, you can chow down, but not now."

She nudged the horse with her heels, brushing back a strand of chestnut-colored hair that had escaped from her ponytail, and the Ghost obediently began to trot.

They were approaching Schoolhouse Lane, the road that joined Orchard Lane where Animal Inn was located, when Val saw a little cart pulled by a burro coming toward them. She knew immediately who it was — Miss Maggie Rafferty driving her fat little donkey, Pedro.

Miss Maggie was somewhere around eighty-five years old, and she was one of the richest people in Essex. But you'd never know it to look at her. She always wore men's trousers tucked into high-topped work boots, and a man's baggy shirt with the sleeves rolled up. Her long, gray-streaked brown hair was twisted into an untidy knot on top of her head, and her eyes were an incredibly bright shade of blue. A lot of people in town thought Miss Maggie was peculiar because she never spent any of her money on herself and she always said exactly what she thought. But Miss Maggie was one of Val's special friends — she loved animals every bit as much as Val did, and her big old mansion was always full of strays that the Humane Society didn't have room for in their shelter.

Val waved and Miss Maggie waved back. When they met in the middle of the road, The Ghost touched noses with Pedro. The burro's long, furry ears, usually pricked forward in anticipation of a new adventure, were drooping today, and Miss Maggie looked worried. Val thought that was strange. Even stranger was the fact that Miss Maggie's German shepherd, Ludwig, wasn't sitting on the seat beside her.

"Hi, Miss Maggie," Val said. "You're certainly out early this morning."

"I'm always up and about by this hour," Miss Maggie said briskly. "Best time of the day. Guess you think so, too, right?"

Val nodded, smiling, "I sure do." She looked down at the burro. "Pedro doesn't look very happy, though. What's wrong with him? And where's Ludwig?"

Miss Maggie heaved a sigh. "To tell you the

4

truth, Val, I don't know where Ludwig is, and neither does Pedro. That's why he's looking peaked. Ludwig's his best friend and he misses him."

"Did Ludwig run away?" Val asked, surprised.

"Looks like it," Miss Maggie replied. "I let him out for a run last night and he didn't come back. And that's just not like Ludwig. Ever since I adopted him after that fire burned down the Humane Society shelter, he's been a real homebody. But now he's gone, and Pedro and I have been looking all over for him."

"Gee, that's too bad." Val felt very sorry for Pedro — and for Miss Maggie. "Maybe you ought to put up some signs around town," she suggested. "Then if anybody finds him, they can let you know."

"I plan to," Miss Maggie told her. "I have notices right here in the cart, with my phone number and Animal Inn's. I'm out a lot, and if someone finds Ludwig and can't reach me, they can leave a message with Pat Dempwolf." Pat was Animal Inn's receptionist. "I figured young Theodore wouldn't mind."

Val couldn't help smiling to hear her father called "young Theodore." "He wouldn't mind at all," she said. "And I'll keep my eyes open, too. If I see Ludwig, I'll bring him straight home, I promise."

Miss Maggie nodded. "You do that." She jiggled the reins and clucked to Pedro, but the little burro just stood there, hanging his head.

"Come on, Pedro," Val urged. "Ludwig will come back, I'm sure of it."

But Pedro didn't budge.

The Ghost began to fidget, eager to be on his way, and Val patted him, wishing she could so something to cheer the donkey up.

"Now you listen to me, Pedro," Miss Maggie said firmly. "How are we going to find Ludwig if you keep standing here in the middle of the road? We have to go to town and put up these notices. Giddyap, Pedro. *Move!*"

Not even a sad, stubborn donkey could disobey Miss Maggie when she used her schoolteacher voice. She had kept several generations of Essex students in line including Val's father, Dr. Theodore Taylor, with that very same tone. Slowly, Pedro put one hoof in front of the other and started plodding down the lane. But his ears were still drooping.

Val watched as the cart trundled away and finally disappeared around a bend in the road. "I sure hope somebody finds Ludwig," she said to The Ghost. "He's an awfully nice dog, and Miss Maggie and Pedro are very fond of him." She nudged her horse gently with her heels and he broke into a trot, heading for Animal Inn.

Suddenly Val had an idea. "I think I'll wait till Toby shows up for work," she told The Ghost. "I'll ask him to be on the lookout for Ludwig, and to ask his brothers for their help, too."

Toby Curran was another of Doc Taylor's young

helpers at Animal Inn. During the summer, he worked there on Val's days off, so they didn't see much of each other, and Val kind of missed him. Toby was fourteen, only a year older than she, and they were good friends. He knew a lot about animals, especially cows, because his father owned Curran's Dairy Farm. But unlike Val, Toby didn't plan on becoming a vet.

As Val and The Ghost came down Schoolhouse Lane and turned onto Orchard, Val saw Toby's bike leaning next to hers against the white fence that surrounded her father's Small Animal Clinic.

"Oh, good! Toby's here early!"

She dismounted by the barn, led The Ghost inside, and took off his saddle and bridle. Then she gave him a quick rubdown and let him out into the pasture behind the Large Animal Clinic. Before Val went to talk to Toby, she gave her horse the carrots she'd brought for him and hugged him. Pleased with carrots — and the hug — The Ghost snorted his thanks and trotted off, kicking up his heels like a colt instead of the fifteen-year-old he actually was. Smiling, Val started off to find Toby.

He was in the clinic's new boarding kennel, giving the cats and dogs their breakfast. When Toby saw Val, he said, "Hey, what are you doing here? This is your day off, remember?"

"Sure I remember." Val picked up an empty dish

and filled it with kibble from one of the bags of dry dog food. "I just came back from riding The Ghost. Whose dish is this, anyway?"

"That's Oliver Fishel's," Toby told her, and Oliver, a shaggy tan-and-white dog with big, furry paws, barked hungrily. Oliver's owners were on vacation somewhere in New England. At first, he'd missed them a lot, but now he was enjoying his stay at Animal Inn and the company of other dogs and cats.

Val opened Oliver's big, roomy cage, patted him, and put his bowl of food down next to his rawhide bone. As Oliver dug into his breakfast, she said to Toby, "I ran into Miss Maggie this morning, Toby. She was driving Pedro, looking for Ludwig."

"Looking for him? Why? Where was he?"

Val sighed. "If she had known where he was, she wouldn't have been looking for him! Ludwig's missing. He ran away."

Toby was as surprised as Val had been. "You're kidding. Ludwig ran away? What would he do a thing like that for? He was so happy with Miss Maggie."

"I thought so, too," Val said. "And so did Miss Maggie and Pedro. Pedro's real upset — Ludwig's his best friend. Miss Maggie's upset, too, though she doesn't show it. She's going to put notices up all over town. I told her I'd look for him, and I thought maybe you and your brothers would help me."

Toby nodded. "Sure. Even though Jake's just a

little kid, he gets around. And since Luther drives he'll be able to cover a lot of territory. If any of us spot old Ludwig, we'll let you know."

"Thanks, Toby." Val smiled. "I knew I could count on you."

Toby finished feeding Spike Spangler, a fiesty wirehaired terrier. Then he and Val went into the waiting room. As Toby picked up the clipboard with Doc's notes on the medications that were to be given, he said, "I bet we won't have to look very hard. Ludwig always wears that red collar Miss Maggie bought him, and it has tags with his name and address. Somebody's probably found him already."

"I hope so," Val said. Then she frowned. "But Ludwig was a stray — that's why he ended up at the Humane Society shelter. What if he just decided to go back to his real home, wherever that is, and his owners recognized him and took off his collar?"

"Hey, Val, you're not thinking straight. If his real owners want him back, then that's where he belongs. He's *their* dog, not Miss Maggie's," Toby pointed out with infuriating logic.

Val hadn't thought of that, and now that she did, she didn't like it one bit. "But that wouldn't be fair. Miss Maggie adopted him so he belongs to *her*."

"Not if he wants to live with his real owners," Toby said. "Besides, Miss Maggie has lots of other dogs and cats, too. What's the big deal?"

"The big deal is that Ludwig is Pedro's best

friend, and he's miserable without him," Val said hotly. "Pedro might pine away and *die* if Ludwig doesn't come back! And if Pedro dies, Miss Maggie will be awfully sad. Even though she doesn't look it, Miss Maggie's very old. She might get so sad that *she'll* pine away and die, too!"

Toby groaned. "Gimme a break, Val! First you ask me to help you look for a lost dog, and that's okay. Then all of a sudden you're talking about a dead donkey and a dead old lady! What's with you, anyhow?"

"Toby Curran, you don't have any more feeling than — than that bench!" Val snapped, gesturing at one of the seats in Animal Inn's waiting room.

"Well, if you ask me, *you* have too *much* feeling!" Toby snapped back.

"I *didn't* ask you!" Val shouted. Some friend Toby had turned out to be!

"What's going on here? Have I just come in on the beginning of World War Three?"

Flushed with anger, Val turned to see her father coming into the waiting room. Though his expression was solemn, Doc Taylor's eyes were twinkling as he looked from her to Toby.

"Uh . . . no, Dad," Val said, thrusting her hands into the pockets of her jeans. "Toby and I were just having a little argument, that's all."

"So I heard." Doc came over to her and kissed her cheek. "Missed you at breakfast, honey. But I guess you had more important things to do, like fighting with Toby."

Val scowled. "It didn't start out to be a fight, but Toby said — "

"Val said — " Toby began.

"Hold it!" Doc raised one hand, and they fell silent. "Would somebody like to tell me in plain English what the problem is?"

Val looked at Toby and Toby looked at Val. At last Val spoke. "Miss Maggie Rafferty's dog is missing, and I asked Toby to help me look for him, that's all. But Toby — "

"Which dog?" Doc asked. "Miss Maggie has a lot of them."

"Ludwig," Toby said. "That German shepherd she adopted after the fire. Val was riding The Ghost this morning, and — "

"And I met Miss Maggie and Pedro," Val cut in. "Miss Maggie told me she was looking for Ludwig because he ran away last night. So I said I'd look, too, and then — "

"And then she asked me and my brothers to help her, and I said we would," Toby interrupted. "That's when Val started yelling at me."

Val glared at him. "That's not true, Dad. I didn't start yelling at Toby until I found out that he doesn't care if Miss Maggie and Pedro get sick and die of grief if they can't find Ludwig!"

"You're bananas, you know that?" Toby said.

Before Val could speak, Doc put a hand on her shoulder. "I think I'm beginning to get the picture and it's a pretty silly one. Vallie, calm down. As far as I know, both Miss Maggie and that little burro are in perfect health. It's unlikely that either of them will die because of a missing dog, no matter how much they love him. I'm sure Ludwig will turn up sooner or later — no need to get all upset about it."

"That's exactly what I told her," Toby said smugly.

Val wanted to stick out her tongue at him, but she knew that would be childish, so she didn't. Besides, she was beginning to feel a little foolish for blowing up the way she had.

"I don't see that there's anything to argue about," Doc said. He looked down at Val. "Aren't you and Jill supposed to be going on a picnic today?"

"Well, yes, but not until later," Val said. "And I was so worried about Ludwig . . ."

"He'll show up," her father assured her. "And even if he doesn't, Miss Maggie and Pedro will survive, believe me. Why don't you go home now, Vallie? You can look for Ludwig along the way."

"Miss Maggie put Animal Inn's phone number on the notices she's putting up," Val mumbled. "I guess you better tell Pat when she gets in so she knows what to say if anyone calls."

"I'll tell her," Toby volunteered. He smiled at her just a little. "No hard feelings?"

After a moment, Val smiled, too. "No hard feelings. I'm sorry I yelled at you."

Toby's smile widened into a grin. "So am I! I'll let you know if Jake and Luther or me find Ludwig."

Doc put his other hand on Toby's shoulder. "How about shaking hands?"

Val and Toby eyed each other. Then Val stretched out her hand and Toby shook it vigorously.

Doc leaned down and kissed Val's cheek — his short gray beard tickled a little. "Have a nice picnic, honey. See you tonight."

"You call me if you find Ludwig, okay?" Toby said.

Val nodded. "Okay." She hurried out of the waiting room, heading for her bike.

Chapter
2

Instead of taking York Road, the most direct route to the center of town, Val biked down a series of side streets. She rode very slowly, looking everywhere for Ludwig. Sometimes she even called, "Here, Ludwig! Here, boy!" but people in their yards or on their way to work eyed her strangely when she did that, so she stopped. Although she saw many dogs as she rode along, none of them were Ludwig.

Turning onto Market Street in downtown Essex, Val stopped for a red light and glanced around. Miss Maggie had done her work well — there was a notice about the missing dog fastened to every tree and parking meter along the street. Val got off her bike and walked over to read one of them.

LOST DOG, it said, in Miss Maggie's schoolteacher script. GERMAN SHEPHERD. ANSWERS TO THE NAME LUDWIG. WEARING RED COLLAR AND I.D. TAGS WHEN LAST SEEN. IF FOUND PLEASE CALL MARGARET RAFFERTY, 243-7811. IF NO ANSWER CALL ANIMAL INN, 249-6023 AND LEAVE MESSAGE. Miss Maggie certainly hadn't wasted any words, but then she never did.

Val was about to get back on her bike when she saw another sign taped to the window of Kane's Kandy Store, right above the display of daily newspapers. This one read, REWARD!!! MY VERY VALUABLE HIMALAYAN CAT NAMED PUFFIN HAS BEEN MISSING SINCE AUGUST 7TH!!! That was the day before yesterday. Val read on. PUFFIN HAS LONG SILKY FUR LIKE A PERSIAN, BUT SHE IS MARKED LIKE A SIAMESE AND SHE HAS BEAUTIFUL GOLDEN EYES. I AM HEARTBROKEN!!! PUFFIN ALWAYS WEARS AN ADORABLE TURQUOISE-BLUE COLLAR STUDDED WITH RHINESTONES!!! IF YOU FIND HER, PLEASE CALL 243-6974!!! There was a photograph of Puffin attached to the sign. Val recognized the cat immediately. Her owner, Mrs. Elsie Van Fleet, was one of Animal Inn's clients, and she brought Puffin every other week to their new grooming salon to be shampooed, blow-dried, and fluffed. As far as Val knew, Puffin was never allowed to set paw outside the Van Fleets' house except for her trips to Animal Inn. Puffin was definitely not the sort of cat who would stray. Yet she was missing, like Ludwig.

As Val wheeled her bike across the intersection, she saw Miss Maggie's cart and Pedro up ahead. Pedro was tied to a parking meter, hanging his head and looking sad, but Miss Maggie was nowhere in sight.

Coming up next to him, Val patted Pedro's furry head. "Hi, Pedro. Long time no see," she joked. Pedro gave her a sorrowful look, as though to say

15

that he wasn't in the mood for humor.

"Hey, Pedro, lighten up," Val urged, scratching behind his drooping ears. Remembering that she still had one carrot left, she took it out of her jeans pocket and offered it to the little burro. But Pedro just sniffed at it and sighed. Maybe he *would* pine away and die, Val thought. Pedro usually loved carrots. Val sighed, too.

"Hello again, Val Taylor!" Miss Maggie had just marched out of the bank building near where Pedro was tethered. She had a lot of notices in her hand. "I just spoke to Mr. Nace, the bank manager — told him I needed to use his copying machine to make more signs because I was running low. He was very obliging." She grinned at Val. "As well he should be! He can't risk offending one of his biggest depositors. There's something to be said for having more money than you know what to do with." Miss Maggie thrust a handful of notices at Val. "Here — put some of these up for me. Got any thumbtacks?"

"Uh . . . no, not with me," Val said.

"Well, I do. Have some." Miss Maggie dug into a shirtpocket and dropped some tacks into Val's outstretched hand. "I don't suppose you've seen hide nor hair of Ludwig? No, of course you haven't or you would have said so — if I'd let you get a word in edgewise, that is."

Val shook her head. "No, I haven't, but I'm going to keep on looking, and so are Toby and his

16

brothers. Did you see the signs about Mrs. Van Fleet's cat, Puffin? She's missing, too."

Miss Maggie snorted. "I did indeed. Knowing Elsie Van Fleet, she's probably simply *mislaid* that poor cat. Ever been in her house?" Without waiting for Val to reply, she went on, "It wouldn't surprise me if she lost *Victor* in there one of these days! Then no doubt she'd put up notices saying, 'Missing — one husband.' " Miss Maggie's bright blue eyes sparkled with mischief, and Val wondered why she had ever thought for even a minute that the testy old woman was in danger of dying from grief.

"Well, I must be on my way," Miss Maggie said, untying Pedro from the parking meter and glancing at the dial. "Hmmm — forty-five minutes left. Why doesn't Essex install those meters that allow one to pay for half an hour at a time? I must speak to the mayor about it." She climbed into the cart and clucked to Pedro. The donkey began to move very slowly down Market Street as Miss Maggie called over her shoulder to Val, "If you run out of thumbtacks, buy some more at the dime store and send me the bill!"

It took over an hour to post all the notices Miss Maggie had given her, and when she finished, Val felt very hot and sticky. She was looking forward to a nice long shower when she got home. Then she'd pack a picnic lunch and go over to Jill's house. On the way to their favorite spot by the lake, they could both keep an eye out for Ludwig — and Puffin. Val didn't really think Mrs. Van Fleet's cat was somewhere in the house. Nobody's house could be *that* messy!

When she reached the Taylors' house on Old Mill Road, Val leaned her bike against the apple tree in the backyard and went in the back door. Jocko, the shaggy little black-and-white mongrel, and Sunshine, the big golden retriever, came running to meet her, tails wagging furiously.

"Hey, guys, I've only been gone for a few hours," she said, laughing and petting them.

"*Mrrrow?*" said Cleveland, Val's big orange cat. He was sitting on the kitchen counter, waiting for her to finish paying attention to the dogs and give him a cuddle. Val scooped him up and tickled him under the chin, but he didn't purr. Cleveland never purred when Mrs. Racer was vacuuming, and she was doing that now in the living room. Mrs. Racer was the Taylors' elderly Mennonite housekeeper, but she was just like a member of the family. Since Mrs. Taylor's death in an automobile accident three years ago, Mrs. Racer had taken care of all of them, running the household with efficiency and love.

With Cleveland in her arms and the dogs frisking around her feet, Val went through the dining room and into the living room. Mrs. Racer, her silvery hair in a neat bun under the white lawn cap she always

18

wore, a white apron over her simple cotton dress, was so busy vacuuming that she didn't notice Val.

"Hi, Mrs. Racer," Val shouted over the noise of the motor. Then, "*Ouch!*" she squawked, as Cleveland's claws dug into her shoulder as he struggled to escape. Cleveland had hated the vacuum cleaner ever since Val had once used it on him when he was shedding. She let him go, and Jocko and Sunshine tore off in pursuit of the terrified cat, nearly knocking Mrs. Racer down.

"You leave Cleveland alone!" Mrs. Racer cried, but neither of the dogs paid any attention. She saw Val and turned off the vacuum. "Oh, hello, Vallie. When did you come home?"

"Just a few minutes ago," Val said. "Did Teddy and Erin get off all right?"

"Sure they did," Mrs. Racer said. "Teddy was already gone by the time m'son Henry dropped me off, and Erin's friend's mother picked her up right on time to go to that fancy ballet class over in Carlisle."

Erin was a very talented dancer. She wanted to be a ballerina like her mother, who had been a dancer with the Pennsylvania Ballet before marrying Doc. This summer, Erin had been accepted into a special program for young dancers on the campus of Cumberland College in the nearby town of Carlisle. Her best friend, Olivia, had been accepted, too, and Olivia's mother drove them and brought them home every day.

"Oh, good," Val said. "I left early to take The Ghost for a ride. That's why I wasn't here to see them off."

Mrs. Racer smiled at her. "Now, Vallie, don't you worry about them kids. Between your pop and me, they're going to be just fine. You're supposed to be taking it easy for a change — Doc told me so. 'Don't let Vallie get all *ferhoodled* about Teddy and Erin,' he told me. 'She worries about 'em too much,' he said. 'She's just a kid, too. Time she enjoyed herself.' And he's right, Vallie. Your pop is always right."

"I know," Val said, smiling. "And I *am* enjoying myself, honest. Jill and I are going on that picnic today, down by Muskrat Lake. But first, I have to take a shower and change my clothes. I got all sweaty, biking around town and putting up notices about Miss Maggie's missing dog. Her German shepherd, Ludwig, ran away last night."

"Ludwig — isn't that the dog Miss Maggie adopted after the big fire?" Mrs. Racer asked. "The one she got around the same time she bought that poor little donkey that was bein' treated so mean?"

"That's the one," Val said.

Just then the clock on the mantel chimed half past eleven.

"Oh, wow! I have to hurry if I'm going to meet Jill at noon."

As she started for the stairs, Mrs. Racer said,

"I've fixed you a nice picnic lunch, Vallie. There's potato salad left over from last night and I made you a couple of sandwiches. I know you like egg-and-olive. And peanut butter and jelly . . . but just in case I also made tuna fish." Mrs. Racer knew that Val didn't eat meat. "How about a tomato from the garden? I picked a beauty this morning. And a thermos full of lemonade, and some brownies, and a few oatmeal-raisin cookies. . . ."

"That sounds like *three* lunches," Val laughed. "Thanks, Mrs. Racer. I'll be down in about fifteen minutes."

It took longer than fifteen minutes though, for Val to wash and change, mostly because Jocko ran off with one of her sneakers. She had to chase him all through the house until she got it back, so by the time she packed the enormous lunch Mrs. Racer had prepared into her knapsack, got on her bike and rode over to Jill's, it was almost twenty after twelve. Val expected to see Jill out in front of the house, tapping her foot impatiently — Jill was always on time for everything and couldn't understand why other people couldn't always be prompt, too.

But she wasn't waiting out front, so Val rang the bell and then opened the front door, calling, "Jill? It's me, Val. Sorry I'm late — sorry, sorry, sorry!" When Jill didn't answer, Val started wandering through the downstairs looking for her. She walked on tiptoe, not wanting to leave dirty footprints on the Dearbornes' pale green carpet. Jill's mother was an interior decorator, and everything in the house was absolutely perfect, like an ad in a magazine. It was *completely* unlike the Taylors' comfortable, slightly shabby home. Val had often thought that was why Jill spent so much time at Val's house. Besides, she was an only child, and she enjoyed being treated like another sister by Teddy and Erin and playing with all the Taylors' pets. Jill's parents had agreed to only one pet — a half-grown calico kitten named Patches that Jill had adopted from a litter left on the Taylors' doorstep.

Val stuck her head into the kitchen, thinking that Jill might have been fixing her lunch and hadn't heard Val or the bell. But Jill wasn't there, though her knapsack was on the counter. Seeing that the back door was open, Val stepped out onto the porch.

"Jill!" she shouted. "Where are you?"

"Val? Is that you?" Jill's voice sounded very far away. Looking out over the Dearbornes' big yard, Val saw a small, blonde figure way back by the hedge. Jill was on her hands and knees, peering under the hedges into the neighbors' gardens.

"What are you doing?" Val asked, crossing the velvety lawn to Jill's side. "Lose something?"

Jill stood up, brushing dirt and grass off her knees. She was much shorter than Val, and her fair hair, usually so neat, was straggling around her face

22

in limp wisps. "Patches," she sighed. "That darned cat escaped again and I can't find her. I thought she might have decided to visit the Boyds' cat, but I've been calling and calling and she hasn't showed up. I hate to leave her outside — since your dad declawed her, she can't protect herself if she gets into a fight."

Val grimaced. "I wish your folks hadn't insisted on having Patches declawed," she said. "I know your mom didn't want her to scratch the furniture, but unless a cat *never* goes outside, it needs to be able to fight back if it runs into an enemy."

"Well, Patches isn't *supposed* to go outside, but she does every time we open the door. She's like greased lightning!" Jill put her hands on her hips and yelled, "*Patches*, you come here *this minute*!"

Patches didn't.

"Oh, well." Jill shrugged. "She takes off all the time, and I'm not going to wait around till she comes home. Let's go, Val. Patches will probably be sitting on the doorstep when we get back from our picnic."

The girls went back into the house and Jill picked up her knapsack and slung it over her shoulder. "I don't suppose Mrs. Racer gave you any brownies, did she?" she asked hopefully.

Val grinned. "Enough for an army!" She knew how much Jill loved Mrs. Racer's brownies. "And some oatmeal-raisin cookies, too. What have you got?"

"Weird stuff," Jill said, leading the way to the front door. "Mom and Dad had a party last night, so I got the leftovers — chopped liver, some Italian ham on rye bread with Dijon mustard, and some vegetable glop that has eggplant, tomatoes, and zucchini in it. *They* call it ratatouille, but *I* call it 'rotted tooey!'"

They both giggled. "Rotted tooey sounds terrific," Val said. "You can keep the pig meat and the liver!"

Jill made a face. "I wish you wouldn't call ham 'pig meat,'" she said.

"Well, that's what it is," Val replied. "I'll stick with my egg-and-olive, tuna fish, and peanut butter."

"All in one sandwich? Yuck!" Jill teased.

"No, dopey — *three* sandwiches. Hurry up and get your bike, and let's get going. I can't wait to take a nice, cool swim before lunch."

Jill trotted around the side of the house to the garage where she kept her bike and pedaled up the driveway to join Val. Grinning mischievously, she said, "I forgot to tell you what I brought for dessert — chocolate mousse! I'll trade with you for some brownies and cookies. And don't you dare tell me you don't eat *moose*, either!"

Laughing, the girls headed for Muskrat Lake.

Chapter
3

There was little shade along the two-lane black-top that led to Muskrat Lake, and by the time Val and Jill got there, they were both baking in the hot August sun. They wheeled their bikes down to the water's edge, selecting a spot that was far enough away from other picnickers to be peaceful, yet still within the lifeguard's range. Then they dropped their knapsacks, peeled off the clothes they'd worn over their bathing suits, and plunged into the cold, clear lake.

"Oh, wow! Does that feel good!" Val sighed happily.

"Does it ever!" Jill agreed. "I'm surprised I didn't sizzle when I hit the water, I was so hot."

"Race you to the float," Val sang out, and began swimming with swift, sure strokes. As much as she loved working at Animal Inn, it sure was nice to just goof off for a change, she thought. Maybe on Sunday she'd talk her father into taking the whole family on a picnic to Muskrat Lake — Doc worked harder than anyone she knew, and he deserved some time off, too.

After their swim, the girls dug into their picnic. Val didn't have room for her peanut butter-and-jelly sandwich, so she broke it into little bits and fed the fat, sassy squirrels that scampered around them looking for a handout. Suddenly she saw a big German shepherd racing across the grass and realized guiltily that she'd forgotten all about Miss Maggie's missing dog.

Scrambling to her feet, she shouted, "Ludwig! Jill, come on — I think that's Ludwig Rafferty, and we've got to catch him!"

"What would Ludwig be doing here?" Jill asked puzzled, as she ran after Val. "I don't see Miss Maggie anywhere."

"He ran away last night," Val told her, dodging in and out among blankets, picnic baskets, and startled people. "I told Miss Maggie I'd look for him, and I think I just saw him!"

She ducked just in time to avoid a flying Frisbee, and leaped over an innertube a toddler was pulling out of the water. The German shepherd had now charged over to a family with two small boys, and the older boy was offering him a hot dog. Val dashed over to them, but Jill hung back.

"Val, I don't think . . ." she began.

"Ludwig, is that you?" Val said eagerly.

The father of the family, a thin man wearing

baggy plaid shorts, squinted up at her. "Nobody here by that name, sis," he said. "I think you've got the wrong party."

"I didn't mean you. I was talking to the dog." Val was afraid she sounded rude, so she added, "I've been looking for a German shepherd named Ludwig, and I thought maybe . . ."

"What a funny name for a dog," the man said. "This dog belongs to me, and her name's Lady."

"You mean he's a she? I mean, your dog is a female?" Val asked, disappointed.

The man's wife laughed. "If she's not, then I guess she made medical history when she had her puppies!"

"Oh," Val said in a small voice. "Well, sorry I bothered you. Uh . . . enjoy your picnic." She hurried away. Jill fell into step next to her.

"Honestly, Val!" Jill groaned. "Sometimes you do the most embarrassing things! Those people must think you're some kind of a nut, running up to them like that and talking to their dog."

"But I always talk to dogs," Val said. "I talk to all animals, you know that."

Jill rolled her eyes. "Do I ever!"

"What embarrasses *me* is that in the first place, I ought to have known it wasn't Ludwig, and in the second place, when I got closer, I should have known it was a female. Some vet I'm going to be!"

Giggling, Jill said, "Well, you didn't exactly

27

have time to conduct a thorough examination!''

"True . . .'' Val slowed down and turned back, looking at Lady, who was chasing a stick one of the boys had thrown for her. "I wonder . . .''

"Now what?''

"Oh, I was just wondering who their vet is. Lady's never been to Animal Inn. Maybe I ought to go back and tell them that my father's the best vet for miles around . . .''

Jill groaned again, louder this time. "Val Taylor, you're supposed to be on vacation! Can't you forget about Animal Inn for just a few hours?''

Val glanced at her friend sheepishly, and said, "No, not really. But I'll try.''

"Good,'' said Jill. "Hey, look over there — it's Sarah Jones and Lisa and Nancy. They're waving at us. Let's go say hello.''

"Sure. I've hardly seen them at all this summer.''

Val and Jill went over to join the other girls, classmates of theirs at Alexander Hamilton Junior High. They laughed and talked, comparing notes about their summer while listening to rock music on Sarah's cassette player. Then they swam, meeting some other classmates who were hanging out at the lake. The afternoon passed swifly, and almost before Val knew it, the tall trees that ringed Muskrat Lake were casting long shadows across its grassy banks.

"What time is it, anyway?'' Jill asked. "I told

Mom and Dad I'd be home in time for supper, and I bet it's after five."

"I bet you're right." Val stood up from the blanket where she had been lying and looked around. Most of the families had packed up and left for home. "Guess we'd better get going."

She and Jill said good-bye to their friends and headed back to the spot where they had left their knapsacks and bikes. They gathered up their belongings, wheeled their bikes up to the road, and began pedaling back to Essex.

Seeing the traffic that whizzed by on the main road, Val said, "Let's take a short cut. If we make a right at Spring Valley Road, we'll get home faster, and we won't have to worry about all these cars."

"Whatever you say," Jill replied. "The faster the better. My folks expect me to be there when they get home from work."

They had gone less than a mile on the back road when Val saw something that made her slow her bike to a stop. Jill pulled up beside her and stopped, too. They both stared at a sign that stood next to a paved driveway leading from the road. Both the sign and the driveway looked very new.

" 'Spring Valley Research Laboratory,' " Val read aloud. "That sign wasn't here the last time I came this way."

"I wonder what kind of research they do," Jill said.

"Let's find out," Val suggested. "It can't hurt to ride up this drive and see what's going on. *Please,* Jill."

"Well . . . okay." Jill looked at her watch. "If I'm home by six, that'll be all right."

The drive led to a long, low building made of fresh blond wood with lots of windows. Flowering plants had been set out in the beds surrounding it. Like everything else, the plants looked very new — they were very small, with more buds than flowers. The lawn was even newer. It was the kind of lawn that comes ready-made in strips of bright green sod. Val could clearly see the seams between one strip and another as she got off her bike and walked up to the entrance of the building.

"Val, what're you *doing*?" Jill whispered nervously, staying where she was. "I don't think you ought to go so close. Maybe this is some kind of top-secret laboratory, like in the movies. There might be guards, or something."

"If it was top-secret, there'd be a big wall all around it, with signs saying 'Keep Out — No Trespassing,' " Val pointed out. She leaned her bike against one of the square wooden pillars that stood on either side of the tall glass doors, pressing her nose to the glass and peering inside. All she saw was a large entrance hall with a few modern couches, a shiny marble floor, and some abstract paintings on the walls. There was nobody in sight. She returned to her bike and began wheeling it back to where Jill stood halfway down the driveway, looking anxious.

"Nothing to see," Val said. "But it's kind of strange, a place like this way out in the middle of nowhere."

"Val, let's go home, okay? This place gives me the creeps!"

But Val had noticed a high fence made of cedar posts behind the building. "I wonder what's behind that fence?" she said.

"Probably nuclear reactors or something, like at Three Mile Island!" Jill was getting more nervous by the minute.

Suddenly from behind the fence came the loud barking of large, angry dogs.

"I told you so!" Jill mounted her bike and began riding at top speed down the drive. "They've got guard dogs! I bet there's an electric eye kind of thing that tells them when somebody's snooping around, and if we don't go away, they'll attack us!"

"You watch too many dumb movies," Val said. But she got onto her bike, too, and followed Jill down the drive to Spring Valley Road. When she caught up with her, she said, "I'll ask Dad if he knows anything about this place. He knows everything that's going on around Essex."

"I don't like it," Jill said, pedaling furiously. "I don't like it one bit!"

Chapter 4

The minute Val came into the house, she was greeted by the dogs, Cleveland, and Teddy, who dashed into the hall shouting, "Hey, Vallie, wanna hear a new joke?" He was wearing nothing but a pair of rumpled shorts and his beloved Phillies baseball cap because it was still so hot, even though it was after six o'clock.

"Sure," Val said, dropping her knapsack on the hall table. "No, Cleveland," she told the cat, bending down to stroke his fur. "No *way* am I going to pick up something as big and furry as you tonight!"

"Vallie, you listening? It's a real good joke. Sparky told it to me today at camp." Teddy danced ahead of her into the living room. "Okay — ready?"

Val nodded.

"What weighs five hundred pounds, is yellow, and sings?"

Val knew the answer, but she didn't want to spoil his fun. "I give up. What is it?"

"Two two-hundred-fifty-pound canaries!" Teddy whooped with laughter, and Val laughed, too.

"That's a good one, Teddy," she said. "Maybe you ought to tell it to Dandy. I bet he'd go on a diet right away!"

"*My* canary is *not* fat," Erin shouted from where she was standing in front of the electric fan. In her sleeveless pale blue leotard, she looked pretty and cool. Then she giggled. "Maybe you should tell it to him anyway, Teddy. He doesn't get to hear many bird jokes!"

Val joined her sister in front of the fan. "Mmm, this feels so good. Where are Dad and Mrs. Racer?"

"M'son Henry picked Mrs. Racer up right before you came home," Teddy said, flopping down on the floor in front of the television. "And Dad's out back, trying to make the sprinkler work. It got clogged up or something."

Val, who had taken off her sneakers and socks, nudged Teddy in the ribs with her bare toes. "Teddy, you've got to stop calling Henry 'm'son Henry'! Mrs. Racer always calls him that because he *is* her son. His real name is Henry Racer."

"And you're much too young to have a son, anyway," Erin teased.

"What's for supper, Erin?" Val asked. "I hope it's something cold."

"It is," Erin said. "Mrs. Racer made macaroni salad, pepper slaw, and chicken salad, and sliced tomatoes from the garden with vinegar dressing and basil. And there's watermelon for dessert. Now that you're home, we can eat."

"Terrific! I'm starved." Val took off her T-shirt and tossed it on a chair. She felt much cooler in just her bathing suit and shorts. "I'll go see if I can help Dad with the sprinkler and then I'll help you serve supper."

As Val started through the dining room into the kitchen with Jocko and Sunshine at her heels, Erin called, "D.L.T.D.O!" That was the Taylor family's abbreviation for "Don't Let The Dog Out." Jocko just couldn't resist the sight of an open door. Sometimes he'd be gone for hours until somebody found him, read his name and address on his tags, and brought him home.

"I won't," Val called back. She scooted out the back door, closing it quickly before Jocko could follow her.

"Hi, Dad . . . *oh!*"

A shower of cold water hit her as she came down the steps to the backyard.

"You fixed it!"

"Looks like I did," Doc said, grinning at her. "I'm not sure *what* I did, but it seems to be working. Sorry, honey. I didn't mean to drench you."

Val laughed. "It feels wonderful." Wiping the drops of water from her eyes, she added, "Supper's

34

going to be ready in a few minutes. Are you as hungry as I am?"

"Maybe hungrier. I didn't have any lunch. Have a nice time with Jill this afternoon?"

"Oh, yes. It was really great," Val said. "We ran into some of our friends from school. And we saw a German shepherd that looked like Ludwig Rafferty, but it wasn't. Did anybody call Animal Inn about him today?"

"Not that I know of." Her father came up the steps behind her and they both went into the kitchen. "Mrs. Van Fleet called about her missing cat, though. She wants me to tell Sheriff Weigel that Puffin's been kidnapped and is being held for ransom. Apparently the sheriff didn't take her seriously when she called him herself."

"Somebody kidnapped a cat?" Erin asked as she set a bowl of chicken salad on the butcher block table.

"Mrraow?" Cleveland added from his usual perch on the kitchen counter.

"Oh, wow!" Teddy, who had just finished feeding the dogs, ran over to Doc. "Did they send a ransom note and everything? Are they asking for thousands and thousands of dollars?"

Doc laughed. "No, Teddy, nothing like that. There *is* no ransom note, but Mrs. Van Fleet is expecting one any minute. In the meantime, she's offering a hundred-dollar reward to anyone who finds Puffin.''

"Oh, boy! Wait'll I tell Sparky and Eric and Billy! I bet we can find Mrs. Van Fleet's dumb old cat, and then we can split the reward. Let's see — that's twenty-five dollars each. Wow! What does she look like?''

"Mrs. Van Fleet? Well, she's about my age, about five feet four . . .'' Doc teased.

"Not her! Her cat — Puddin' or whatever its name is,'' Teddy giggled.

"Her name's Puffin, and she's a Himalayan. She looks like a long-haired Siamese with a kind of pushed-in face,'' Val said, filling four glasses with lemonade. "And she was wearing a turquoise collar with rhinestones.''

"Poor Mrs. Van Fleet,'' Erin said. "She must be awfully worried.''

"So's Miss Maggie. Ludwig's lost, too,'' Val told her. "I helped her put up signs about him all over town this morning.''

"How much of a reward is Miss Maggie gonna give?'' Teddy asked eagerly. "If me and my friends find 'em both, we'll be rich!''

Val frowned at him. "I don't think Miss Maggie is offering a reward, Teddy. Anyway, money's not important. The important thing is to find Ludwig and Puffin so their owners won't be all upset.''

"Vallie's right.'' Doc sat down at the table. "If

either you or Erin happen to find the animals, you'll be making two nice people very happy."

"You'll be making a nice burro very happy, too," Val said as she, Teddy, and Erin took their places. "Pedro's awfully sad without his friend."

"Poor Miss Maggie — and poor Pedro," Erin sighed.

"And poor me — if I don't have something to eat right now, there'll be nothing left of me but a skeleton. And you don't want a skeleton for a father, do you?" Doc said, reaching for the macaroni salad. "Vallie, pass your plate. Erin, how about you? Teddy, think you can serve the chicken salad without dumping it on the floor?"

Over supper, everyone talked about what they had done during the day. Teddy had been promoted from a Tadpole to a Bluefish in his swimming class at day camp; Erin was full of stories about rehearsal for the ballet program's final recital; Doc told them about some of his animal patients; and Val suggested that they all take a picnic to Muskrat Lake on Sunday.

"Speaking of Muskrat Lake," she said as she helped Erin clear the table, "Jill and I took a short cut on the way home this afternoon. We went down Spring Valley Road, and we discovered something interesting. Dad, do you know anything about the Spring Valley Research Laboratory? It's a brand new building with a big sign out front, but it doesn't say what kind of research they do."

Teddy's eyes widened. "Hey, cool! Maybe there's a mad scientist like Dr. Frankenstein who's gonna make a really neat monster!"

"Teddy, you've got to stop watching all those horrible movies on TV," Erin said with a delicate shudder.

"They're *horror* movies, not horrible movies," Teddy said. "And I hardly watch 'em at all 'cause Dad won't let me."

"Jill thinks they do some kind of nuclear research," Val added. "That could be more dangerous than Frankenstein's monster!"

Doc got up and began loading the dishwasher. "As a matter of fact, I was reading something about the Spring Valley lab in the paper the other day. Sorry to disappoint you, Teddy, but they don't make monsters. And they don't do nuclear research either, Vallie, so you can put Jill's mind at ease. It's an animal research laboratory."

Val gasped and stared at her father in horror. "Oh, no! You mean they cut animals up and make them sick and use them for experiments?"

"Vallie, calm down," Doc said. "It's not that kind of place at all. The Spring Valley facility studies animal behavior, to try to find out why animals do what they do, how much they can be taught, and what they can teach us. I meant to save the article for you, but I'm afraid it slipped my mind."

Val was still not convinced. "Maybe that's what

they told the newspaper reporter, but that doesn't mean that's *all* they do. Maybe they do horrible things to animals and they just don't want anybody to know about it.''

Doc sighed. ''Honey, this seems to be your day for making mountains out of molehills. The *Essex Gazette* is a thoroughly reliable paper with thoroughly professional reporters. If there was anything fishy going on at the Spring Valley lab, they would have ferreted it out.''

''Hey, Dad, you just made a good joke,'' Teddy said, grinning. ''You said if there's something *fishy*, the reporters would've *ferreted* it out. Get it?'' he added when Doc looked blank. ''You were talking about animals, and then you said *fishy* and *ferret* . . .''

''A fish isn't an animal exactly,'' Erin said, taking half a watermelon out of the refrigerator and putting it on the counter.

Teddy frowned at her. ''Well, it's funny anyway, so there!''

''Glad you think so, Teddy,'' Doc said, smiling. He turned to Val. ''But I wasn't trying to be funny, Vallie. I was making a point.''

''I got the message,'' Val said. ''If you say they don't torture animals, I believe you.'' She gave a little sigh of relief. ''It would be terrible if it was that kind of lab!''

Doc started slicing the watermelon with a big, sharp knife, putting the slices on the plates she

39

handed him. "Maybe not so terrible," he said. "Though it may seem cruel, experimentation on animals has led to many medical procedures and medicines that have saved millions of human lives. Don't let your emotions get in the way of your good sense."

This was practically the only topic on which Val and her father were not in full agreement, and Val was tempted to argue with him, but the telephone rang before she could speak.

"I'll get it," she said, and went to pick up the phone. "It might be Toby — he said he'd call if he or his brothers found Ludwig."

It was Toby, but neither he nor Jake nor Luther had seen Miss Maggie's German shepherd. He did have some interesting news, though.

"I was talking to Mike Strickler right before I left Animal Inn," Toby told Val. "He was just coming on duty for the night, and you know what he said?"

"No, what?"

"Well, he had lunch at Rose's Diner, like he always does, but Rose wasn't there. And that's very unusual, because she's *always* there. So Mike asked the waitress if Rose was sick, and she said no, Rose was out looking for her dog Popeye. He ran away last night. She'd tied him to a tree in the yard and he slipped right out of his collar."

Val frowned. "That makes two missing dogs and one missing cat."

"And that's not all," Toby said. "Donna Hartman was closing up the beauty parlor . . ."

"Pet grooming salon," Val corrected him automatically.

"Whatever. Anyway, I met her as I was getting on my bike, and she said that Mrs. Schiller's cat had an appointment this afternoon, but Mrs. Schiller cancelled it because she couldn't find him. And then Mr. Corcoran canceled his cocker spaniel's appointment, too. Guess why?"

"Because Corky Corcoran is lost, I bet," Val said. "Toby, that's *three* missing dogs and *two* missing cats!"

"No kidding." Toby's voice sounded sarcastic. "Believe it or not, I can count. You know something, Val? I think there's something weird going on."

"There sure is!" Val was getting worried now. "Maybe Mrs. Van Fleet is right. Maybe somebody *is* kidnapping people's pets. Listen, Toby, if you hear about any more lost animals, call me right away, okay? And if I find out anything, I'll call you."

"Gotcha. Special agent Curran signing off now. Over and out," Toby joked and hung up.

"Three missing dogs and two missing cats?" Erin said as Val sat down at the table. "Do you really think there's a petnapper in Essex, Vallie?"

Teddy's eyes sparkled under the visor of his baseball cap. "Oh, boy! Petnappers! If me and my

41

gang can catch 'em, I bet we'll get a *huge* reward!''

"Just a minute, everybody," Doc said. "Vallie, what exactly did Toby tell you?"

Between bites of her watermelon, Val repeated what Toby had said. "I don't think it's just a coincidence, Dad. I know some people abandon their pets in the summer when they're going on vacation and they don't want to be bothered finding a place for them to stay. But that's not what's happening here. Miss Maggie and Mrs. Van Fleet and the others *love* their animals. I really think somebody's stealing them. Maybe you ought to call the sheriff, like Mrs. Van Fleet said.''

After a moment's thought, Doc said, "I have to admit that it seems peculiar. But consider this, Vallie — people tend to leave their doors and windows open when it's as hot as it's been lately, and it would be very easy for a dog or cat to slip out without anybody noticing. As for Ludwig, we all know that he was a stray, and Miss Maggie gives him the run of her property. He might have simply taken off again. Think about Jocko here.'' He reached down to scratch behind Jocko's ears, and the shaggy little dog wagged his tail happily. "He loves us, but he has the urge to roam. If I called Sheriff Weigel every time Jocko took off, I'd be a laughingstock.''

"But Dad, it's not just *one* dog," Val pointed out. "It's . . .''

"I know — three dogs and two cats." Doc stood

42

up and began piling watermelon rinds on one plate. Erin got a plastic bag from one of the drawers in the counter and held it open while her father slipped the rinds inside to save for Mrs. Racer to make her famous watermelon pickles.

"Tell you what," Doc said as Val took the empty plates and put them in the dishwasher. "If one other animal disappears before tomorrow noon, I'll talk to the sheriff. Okay?"

Val nodded. "Okay! Thanks, Dad. I guess maybe it *could* be a coincidence after all . . ."

The doorbell rang.

"I'll get it!" Teddy shouted, racing out of the kitchen.

A few minutes later he was back, followed by his friend Sparky and her mother, Mrs. Sparks. Sparky's eyes were red and swollen, and even her stubby pigtails seemed to be drooping — like Pedro's ears that morning. Mrs. Sparks looked very upset.

"Hey, Dad, listen to this!" Teddy said. He looked upset, too. "Go on, Sparky. Tell my dad about Charlie."

Sparky wiped her runny nose with the back of her hand, then wiped her hand on her shorts. "Charlie . . ." She gulped. "Charlie's *gone*! When I got home from camp, Mrs. Wilson, she's our housekeeper . . ."

Doc nodded. "I know." Mrs. Sparks worked in a law office in town, and Mrs. Wilson took care of

43

Sparky and her beloved cat, Charlie, when she was away.

"Mrs. Wilson said she let Charlie out because he was yelling a lot, and he's an indoor-outdoor cat so he goes out all the time but he always comes back and this time he didn't. He's been gone for hours and *hours*!" Sparky wailed.

"Charlie never stays away this long," Mrs. Sparks said, putting her arm around Sparky. "I hate to disturb you, Dr. Taylor, but ever since you saved Charlie from dying of feline leukemia, Sparky thinks you can work miracles." She smiled a little. "I guess I do, too. That's why we're here — to find out if you can pull another miracle out of the hat and give us some idea of how we can find Charlie. Frankly, I'm quite concerned. I saw the notices about Miss Rafferty's dog and Mrs. Van Fleet's cat, and then today my boss told me his dog disappeared last night. When his son went out to give King his breakfast, the doghouse was empty. Several other people I spoke to today are missing pets as well. It's beginning to look — well, peculiar."

Val touched her father's arm. "Dad, you said that if one other animal disappears . . ."

"Won't you come into the living room and sit down?" Doc suggested to Sparky and her mother. "Erin, I believe there's plenty of lemonade left. Why don't you pour some for our guests? I'll be with you in a minute. I think it's time to call Sheriff Weigel."

44

Chapter 5

While Doc spoke to the sheriff, Val helped Erin put tall glasses of lemonade and a plate of Mrs. Racer's oatmeal-raisin cookies on a tray.

"Poor Sparky," Erin said. "She just adores that cat! I hope nothing bad has happened to him or to the other animals. Do you really think somebody's kidnapping them?"

"Shh!" Val said. She was trying to hear Doc's end of the conversation with Sheriff Weigel, but she didn't learn much from what she heard. All Doc said, after he told the sheriff about the missing pets, was "Yes. . . . I see. . . . Yes, that's true. . . . Of course. I'll keep in touch." Then he hung up.

"What did he say, Dad?" Val asked anxiously as Erin took the tray into the living room.

Doc stroked his short, graying beard, frowning. "Well, to tell you the truth, Vallie, he wasn't very helpful. Missing animals aren't very high on his list of priorities, I'm afraid. In his opinion it's not the business of the Essex Police Department to trace lost pets. And I can see his point — they only have five officers and one police car, which happens to have a broken axle at the moment. He suggested that this is a matter for the Humane Society, and I agreed. I'll call the other members of the board tonight."

Angrily, Val said, "That makes me really mad! It's just like when that beautiful collie was hit by a car — if Rex was a person instead of a dog, the police would've tried to find the driver, but they didn't do a thing!"

"I know, honey. But unfortunately there's nothing we can do except to continue to work for animal rights. And we will. But right now, we have to try to make Sparky feel better."

Val and Doc came into the living room. Sparky's mother was sipping her lemonade and talking to Erin, but Sparky herself was curled up in a corner of the sofa, chewing on the end of one pigtail and looking sad.

"Don't you want some of Mrs. Racer's cookies?" Teddy was saying, shoving the plate under Sparky's nose. "They're almost as good as her chocolate chip ones."

But Sparky just shook her head. "I'm not gonna eat *anything* till Charlie comes back," she mumbled.

Mrs. Sparks looked up at Doc. "She didn't eat any supper tonight. I'm really worried about her," she said.

Doc went over to the little girl and sat down next to her. "You know something, Sparky?" he said, taking a cookie from the plate. "Wherever Charlie is, I bet he'd be awfully unhappy if he knew that you weren't eating. And Mrs. Racer would be unhappy, too, if she found out you didn't like her cookies. You don't want to make both Charlie and Mrs. Racer unhappy, do you?"

"N-no," Sparky mumbled around her pigtail.

"You know something else?" Doc said solemnly. "I'm sure this cookie tastes a whole lot better than your hair."

That actually made Sparky smile. "I guess maybe I could eat just one," she said, taking the cookie Doc offered her. "Or maybe two . . ."

"I guess maybe I oughta eat some too, to keep you company," Teddy said. "Watermelon doesn't zackly stick to your ribs."

As Teddy and Sparky munched their cookies, Doc told everyone what Sheriff Weigel had said. "I'll speak to the other board members of the Humane Society and get their thoughts on what we can do," he finished by saying. "In the meantime, Mrs. Sparks, I suggest you and Sparky put up some signs about Charlie, the way Miss Maggie and Mrs. Van Fleet did. You might also place an ad in the Gazette's 'Lost and Found' column, too. And of course, we'll all be on the lookout for Charlie and the other missing animals."

Val bent down and scooped up Cleveland, who had just wandered in from the kitchen and held him close in spite of the heat. "Cleveland, from now on you are an *indoor* cat," she said firmly. "No more running around the neighborhood — I don't want *you* to disappear! I'll tell Mrs. Racer first thing tomorrow not to let you out no matter how loud you yell." All of a sudden, she thought of Jill's kitten, Patches. "Excuse me, everybody," she said, heading for the kitchen with Cleveland still in her arms. "I have to make a phone call!"

Mr. Dearborne answered the phone. "No, Val, Jill's not here right now," he said. "She's out looking for — "

"Patches," Val sighed. "I was afraid of that. Just tell her I called, please. And would you ask her to call me back when she comes home? It's important."

Mr. Dearborne said he would and Val hung up the phone. "Patches is missing, too," she told her cat. "And she doesn't even have claws to defend herself with if some awful person tries to steal her!" She hugged Cleveland so hard that he let out an indignant squawk and struggled to get down. Val let him go and went back into the living room.

Mrs. Sparks and Sparky were getting ready to leave. Sparky had a handful of cookies, but she didn't look happy. "Mom, I don't want to go to camp tomorrow," she said. "I want to stay home and look for Charlie."

"Honey, I don't think . . ." Mrs. Sparks began, but Teddy cut her off.

"Hey, Sparky, that's dumb! You're just one little kid — you'd never find Charlie in a million years. But if you come to camp, me and Billy and Eric'll help you look. We'll get *all* the kids to help you look, and I bet we'll find him, too. And maybe we'll find all the rest of the cats and dogs, and we'll get lots of rewards!" He looked up at Mrs. Sparks. "Are *you* gonna give a reward if somebody finds Charlie?" he asked hopefully.

"Well . . . I hadn't really thought about it," Sparky's mother said. "But now that you mention it . . ."

"Yeah, Mom, why don't you?" Sparky said eagerly. "Then people will look for him real hard! How about ten whole dollars?"

Mrs. Sparks smiled. "We'll see. Come on, Philomena, we really must get home so we can start making up those signs. And I'll put an ad in the paper tomorrow."

"So are you gonna come to camp tomorrow?" Teddy asked his friend. For once he didn't make fun of her real name the way he usually did.

Sparky popped another cookie into her mouth. "I guess. Yeah, I'll come."

"Cool!" Teddy shouted, slapping her on the back. "And tell you what, Mrs. Sparks — if me and my pals find Charlie, you can keep the ten dollars. You can buy him lots and lots of cat food!"

"Thank you, Teddy," Mrs. Sparks said. Her

expression was serious, but Val could see that her eyes were twinkling. "But if you and Sparky and your friends *do* find him, I promise I'll take you all to Curran's Ice Cream Parlor for banana splits." She turned to Doc. "Again, I apologize for bothering you. If you find out anything about these missing pets, please let me know."

"You can count on it."

As Doc showed them to the door, Erin, who had been sitting quietly on the floor patting Jocko and Sunshine, looked up at Val. "What if they *don't* find him, Vallie? What if all those animals really *have* been petnapped?"

Val sat down beside her, stroking Sunshine's golden head. "I don't know. I honestly and truly don't know."

Jill called about an hour later. She sounded close to tears. "I looked *everywhere* for Patches," she said. "And I asked every single person I met, but nobody's seen her. It's like she just vanished into thin air."

"Patches isn't the only one," Val said. "I told you about Ludwig, and over the past few days a lot of other animals have disappeared. Dad's been on the phone for ages, talking to the Humane Society people about it — if you couldn't get through before, that's why."

"What did they say?" Jill asked.

"Not much. Some of their pets are missing, but

they don't know what to do about it except to put ads in the Lost and Found. And when Dad called the sheriff, he wouldn't do anything at all."

"I bet if a lot of *people* were missing, some-body'd do something about it," Jill said. "It's like you're always saying, Val — animals don't have any rights at all!"

"I know." Val sighed. Then she said, "You know what I think? I honestly think there's a petnapper in Essex, and so does Toby. Even Dad agrees that something strange is going on. And you know what else, Jill? I'm beginning to think that the Spring Valley Research Laboratory we passed on the way home today has something to do with it! Dad says they study animal behavior there, and that must mean that they need a lot of animals to study. What I want to know is where do they get the animals they use in their research? What if they sneak around at night *stealing* animals?"

"Oh, Val!" Jill gasped. "That's terrible! I *told* you that place gave me the creeps! Why won't Sheriff Weigel do anything about it? Stealing's against the law."

"The sheriff doesn't know about it because I haven't told Dad what I suspect," Val told her. "Besides, I don't have any proof — yet. If I *did* tell Dad, he'd just say I was making mountains out of molehills again. So what I have to do is get some concrete evidence against those lab people, and the sooner the better, before any more animals are stolen."

"But how are you going to do it?" Jill asked.

"I'm not sure," Val admitted. "I'll think of some way, though. And when I do, I'll let you know."

"Val, you're not going to do anything crazy, are you? I mean, you're not going to try to break into the lab or anything?"

"Of course not. At least, not unless it's absolutely necessary."

Jill thought about that for a moment. "Well, my dad's a lawyer, so if you wind up in jail, I guess maybe he could get you out on bail. Call me tomorrow and let me know what you're going to do, okay?"

"Okay. I'll be working at Animal Inn, so I probably won't be able to call until after we close. And Jill, don't worry too much about Patches. Dad says they don't hurt the animals at Spring Valley lab."

"*If* she's there," Jill said. "But what if she's not?"

"Just don't worry, okay? Talk to you tomorrow."

As Val hung up, she heard Teddy calling to her from his room. "Vallie, aren't you ever gonna tuck me in? You've been on the phone with Jill *forever!*"

"Coming, Teddy." Val headed for her little brother's room.

Teddy was curled up in bed, clutching Fuzzy-

52

Wuzzy, the stuffed toy bear that had been passed from Val to Erin to him. Fuzzy-Wuzzy wasn't fuzzy anymore because all his fur had been snuggled off him long ago, but Teddy didn't mind. He slept with Fuzzy-Wuzzy every night — and with Jocko, who was as usual lying on the floor next to Teddy's bed. His hamsters, John, George, Ringo, and Paula, were taking turns in the wheel in Teddy's Habitrail.

Val sat down on the bed next to Teddy. The heat of the day had been replaced by cool, gentle breezes coming through the bedroom window, promising a cooler tomorrow.

"We're gonna find Charlie, aren't we, Vallie?" Teddy said drowsily. "If me and my pals don't, you will, won't you?"

Tucking his rumpled sheet around him, Val said, "You better believe it. I'm going to find Charlie, and Ludwig, and Puffin, and all the other animals. You go to sleep now, Teddy. Good night, sleep tight . . ."

"Don't let the bedbugs bite. . . ." Teddy's eyelids drooped, but then they opened wide. "Vallie, what's a bedbug?"

Val grinned. "I hope you'll never know. 'Night, Teddy."

" 'Night, Vallie," Teddy mumbled, rolling over and burying his face in his pillow.

Val tiptoed out, picking up the Habitrail on her way so the squeaking of the hamsters' wheel wouldn't wake Teddy up during the night. As she put the plastic cage down on the hall table, she thought about what Teddy had said.

He was sure that the missing animals would be found, and he was counting on her to do it if he and his friends couldn't. She was touched by her little brother's faith in her. But in spite of what she'd told Jill, she wasn't at all sure she could come up with a plan that would get her into the Spring Valley lab. And even if she did, what if the animals weren't there?

The image of Sparky's sad little face and sorrowful Pedro made her wince. Somehow or other, she just had to find those missing pets. Val couldn't wait to tell Toby her suspicions tomorrow morning at Animal Inn — and then she remembered that he wouldn't be there because they were taking turns working.

"Drat!" she muttered. She glanced at her watch. It was still early, not yet nine o'clock. Quickly she dialed the number of the Curran dairy farm. Toby's mother answered.

"Hi, Mrs. Curran. It's Val Taylor. Is Toby there?" she asked eagerly.

"Why, no, Val, he's not," Mrs. Curran said. "He's spending the night with his friend Ralph. They're going fishing early tomorrow morning — I don't expect him back till tomorrow afternoon. Can I take a message?"

Disappointed, Val said, "Well, yes, if you wouldn't mind. Would you please ask him to call me at Animal Inn the minute he comes home? I'll be there all day."

Mrs. Curran said she would, and Val hung up. "Double drat!" she said to the hamsters, who didn't pay any attention at all.

Chapter 6

Val didn't sleep very well that night because she kept waking up and thinking about the missing animals. Finally she dozed off, only to be awakened by the rumble of thunder and flashes of lightning. Moments later, it was pouring. When the thunder subsided, the sound of the rain helped lull her back to sleep.

The storm continued into the morning and she and Doc left for work in the midst of a downpour. But Val didn't mind. Not only had the rain broken the heat wave, but Toby and Ralph wouldn't have been able to go on their fishing trip because of the bad weather. She was right. Around ten o'clock, just as Mr. Bierman had paid his bill and left with Delbert, his half-collie, half-nobody-knew-what dog, Toby came into the waiting room of Animal Inn. He was wearing a yellow slicker, but he didn't have a hat, and water streamed off his wet hair, dripping from his rather big ears.

"What's up?" he said, sloshing over to the reception desk where Val was sitting. Pat Dempwolf had gone on vacation, so Val had to handle the phone in addition to helping her father with his patients. "Mom told me you called last night."

There was nobody in the waiting room, so Val had some free time. She told Toby everything, and as he peeled off his slicker and his socks and sneakers, which were completely soaked, he listened intently.

"Gee, Val, I think you're right," he said. "But I don't think it's the lab people who are stealing all those pets. Maybe there's a middleman, somebody who arranges the kidnapping, then sells the animals to Spring Valley and makes lots of money on the deal."

"Who could it be?" Val asked. "I know just about everybody in Essex. Besides I can't think of anyone that mean!"

"Oh, yeah?" Toby said. "Well, *I* can. My friend Ralph told me something last night that really blew my mind. Listen to this!" He lowered his voice, even though there was nobody around to hear. "Ralph's brother, Steve, is sixteen, and he hangs out with a kind of rough crowd. Those guys will do anything for a buck and they're always asking Steve to go in with them, only Steve won't. But he told Ralph that they've got a really big deal going down, and it has something to do with animals. . . . Do you have a towel or something? The water from my hair is running down my nose."

Val dashed into a treatment room, grabbed a towel, and dashed back, handing it to Toby. He rubbed his wet hair, wiped his face, and said, "That's much better."

"So tell me!" Val cried. "What do these guys want Steve to do?"

"They want him to go somewhere with them tonight, but they won't tell him where or why. All they've told him is that he'll make big bucks, and it has something to do with John Wetzel."

"John Wetzel!" Val gasped. "He's that horrible man who used to own Pedro, and beat him and starved him before Miss Maggie bought him! You're right, Toby — Mr. Wetzel sure is mean. He's just the type who'd do something like this, because it would never occur to him that anybody could really love an animal. And if there's money involved. . . ."

Toby nodded solemnly. "My dad says John Wetzel's a money-grubbing old coot. He'd sell his own grandmother if she wasn't already dead and buried."

"This is even worse than I thought," Val groaned. "Maybe the Spring Valley lab wouldn't hurt the animals, but John Wetzel would. What are we going to do?"

Just then the telephone rang and Val picked it up. "Hello — Animal Inn. May I help you?"

"Pat, that you?" the man at the other end of the line asked. "This here's Bill Parsons. Will you tell

58

Doc I got an emergency? My mare Bella's hurt really bad — she was out in the south pasture and got spooked by lightning — tried to jump the fence. I think her leg's broke. Can Doc come out here right away?"

"I'm sure he can, Mr. Parsons," Val said. "Hold on while I buzz him on the intercom. And it's Val, not Pat — she's on vacation."

She got Doc on the intercom and told him what Mr. Parsons had said.

"I'll be there in a few minutes," Doc said. "You hold the fort while I'm gone. Any patients in the waiting room?"

"No, Dad, but Toby's here, and he told me something about the missing pets that you ought to know — " Val began, but Doc cut her off.

"No time now, honey. Tell me when I get back, okay? Bill Parsons sets great store by that old mare, and I don't want to keep him waiting and worrying.

"Sure, Dad. Talk to you later." Val relayed the message to Mr. Parsons, then hung up the phone.

"Is Mr. Parsons' horse very valuable?" Toby asked.

Val smiled. "She is to Mr. Parsons. Bella's about twenty years old — that's older than The Ghost — and she's got a swayback and an awful disposition, but Mr. Parsons loves her. And speaking of animals people love, how are we going to stop John Wetzel from hurting those stolen pets?"

"Well, I've got a really neat idea," Toby said. His brown eyes were sparkling, and his big ears were pink, the way they always were when he got excited about something. "Listen to this! Ralph's brother doesn't want to get mixed up with Skeeter's gang — Skeeter's kind of their leader — so they'll probably be looking for somebody else to go in with them, right? I'm gonna volunteer!"

"Toby, you're out of your mind!" Val squawked. "You said those guys were rough. You could get hurt if anything went wrong."

"Hey, I'm in great shape." Toby flexed his muscles like a wrestler entering a ring. "I can take anything they dish out."

"Yeah, right. You're going to take on a whole bunch of guys who are bigger and older than you. Come on, Toby, you're not Superman. Besides, your folks wouldn't let you go out late at night with a crowd like that, would they?"

"I could say I was sleeping over at Ralph's again or something," Toby said, scowling.

Val shook her ahead. "No, you couldn't. Forget it. It wouldn't be right, and you know it."

Toby sighed. "I guess. But if I *don't* go, how are we going to find out what's really happening? We don't have any evidence that Skeeter's gang is stealing these animals, or that they're working for Wetzel, or that Wetzel's selling the pets to the Spring Valley lab. And if we don't have evidence, the sheriff will keep right on doing what he's doing now — "

"Which is nothing." Val sighed, too. "And that means that more animals are in danger of being petnapped."

A rumble of thunder made the windows of Animal Inn rattle, and lightning forked outside, narrowly missing one of the overhanging trees. Immediately the lights dimmed and flickered, then brightened again.

"Wow! That was close!" Toby said, peering out one of the windows. "This is some storm, all right. If it keeps up, the gang won't be able to steal any animals tonight. Everyone will be keeping their pets indoors."

"That's one good thing, anyway." Val got up from her seat behind the reception desk and began wandering around the waiting room, too anxious to sit still. "But when the storm's over, they'll start doing it again unless we can stop them. And I don't care what you say, Toby, I'm absolutely *sure* they're doing it."

Suddenly she stopped in her tracks. "Toby, I've got it! Let's go out to Mr. Wetzel's farm!"

"Now?" Toby stared at her. "In all this rain?"

"No, not now, but maybe Friday. Dad has to go to a meeting in Harrisburg that afternoon, so the clinic's only going to be open in the morning. We could meet around one o'clock and bike out to Wetzel's place, kind of check it out to see if any of

61

the animals are there. And if they are, that'll be the evidence we need to convince Sheriff Weigel.''

Toby thought for a minute. ''I hate to admit it, but that's not the worst idea you ever had, Val.'' Then he frowned. ''Why would the animals be at old man Wetzel's farm, though? If he's the brains of the outfit, wouldn't he take them to the lab as soon as the gang stole them?''

Val shook her head. ''I don't think so. Dad told me once that there's a law that says if you find a lost animal and nobody claims it within ten days, it's yours. I bet Mr. Wetzel knows about that law, too. If he sold the animals to the lab the minute he got them, it wouldn't be legal.''

''But it wouldn't be legal anyway, because they're not lost — they're stolen,'' Toby pointed out.

''Yes, but there's no proof of that unless we can come up with something. Toby, do you want to come with me to Wetzel's farm or not?''

''I'll come,'' Toby said. He glanced out the window again. ''Unless it keeps raining cats and dogs.''

Val grinned. ''Cats and dogs is what it's all about!''

The storm lasted for two more days, but began tapering off on Thursday afternoon. By Friday, the sun was shining brightly. As Val biked that afternoon on her way to meet Toby, she remembered the joke Teddy had brought home from day camp last night —

"How do you know that it's been raining cats and dogs? Because the streets are full of poodles!" There were a lot of puddles on Arbor Road, that was for sure. And the dirt road that led to John Wetzel's farm had turned to mud. Val and Toby had to get off their bikes and wheel them along the grassy shoulder, their sneakers squelching with every step.

When they came within sight of the dilapidated buildings, they both stared at the sagging barn and the other sheds and coops that sheltered Mr. Wetzel's stock. Everywhere they looked, they saw peeling paint and rotting clapboards. Even the chickens that were running loose on the sparse grass in front of the weathered farmhouse looked discouraged.

"What a dump!" Toby muttered. "It looks even worse than the last time we were here, when your dad picked up Pedro to take him to Animal Inn."

"It sure does," Val agreed. Her heart sank at the thought that Ludwig, Patches, Puffin, and all of the other missing pets might be hidden away in one of those tumble-down buildings. "Let's check out the barn first — I don't see Wetzel anywhere."

"And his old truck is gone, too. I guess maybe he went into town or somewhere." Toby followed Val down the rutted land to the barnyard. "But what if he comes back? What do we say?"

Val looked over her shoulder at his bike. "We say your bike got a flat tire when we were riding by, and we stopped in to see if he had a bicycle pump."

"But I *don't* have a flat," Toby objected.

"Yes, you do," Val said calmly. "Your front tire's as flat as a pancake."

It was. Toby groaned. "Oh, terrific! What if he comes after us with a shotgun? I won't be able to make a quick getaway!"

"I don't think even Mr. Wetzel would do anything like that," Val said.

"You don't *think*? But what if he does?"

Val stopped in the middle of a puddle. "Toby, if you're scared, you can take my bike and go home right now."

Toby's ears turned bright red. "Me, scared? Of old man Wetzel? Hah! You've got to be kidding!" He strode ahead of her, wheeling his wounded bike. "C'mon, what're you waiting for?"

Val stifled a giggle. "I'm right behind you, Secret Agent Curran!"

The barnyard was a sea of mud, and the big pile of manure steaming in the sun gave off a terrible odor, so they decided to go around back. Leaning their bikes against the barn, they went inside but found it completely empty — and very smelly. Apparently Mr. Wetzel's cows were out in the pasture.

"We'd better take a look at some of the other buildings," Toby said as he and Val came outside, taking deep breaths of the fresh, clean air. "There's a shed over there, behind the chicken coops. Wonder what's in there?"

They started walking toward the shed, and suddenly Val stopped. "Did you hear that?"

"What?"

"Barking! I just heard a dog barking, and it seemed to be coming from the shed." She began to run, and Toby ran, too. "Maybe it's Ludwig! Hurry, Toby!"

They had almost reached the shed, when they heard the sound of an ancient engine behind them. It coughed, growled, and backfired several times.

"Hey, you kids! What are you doing on my property?" a loud voice hollered. "Didn't you see the 'No Trespassing' sign down by the road? I'll get the law on you, you see if I don't!"

Val turned around to see Wetzel leaning out of the window of his truck, a scowl on his lean, nasty face.

"Oh, hi, Mr. Wetzel," Val said brightly. "We didn't see any sign. My friend Toby and I were just looking for somebody who'd let us use a bicycle pump. Toby's bike has a flat. . . ."

Mr. Wetzel stopped his old pickup and got out of the cab, slamming the door just in time to prevent his big, mangy dog.from jumping out, too. The dog bared its yellow teeth and growled menacingly.

"I know who you are," Wetzel said, peering at Val. His grimy overalls and sweat-stained shirt smelled every bit as bad as the barnyard, she thought, and stepped back a pace. "You're Doc Taylor's daughter. I remember you from when your pop stole that burro from me awhile back.''

"He did *not* . . .'' Val began angrily, but now Wetzel was glowering at Toby.

"And I remember you, too — Bill Curran's kid. Think you're somethin' special just because your pop's a rich dairy farmer, doncha? Well, let me tell you somethin', kid. On my land, you ain't nothin' but a trespasser, and this here girl is, too. Now you and your girlfriend get outa here pronto, 'fore I let Champ outa my truck. Champ knows what to do with trespassers!''

Toby clenched his fists and stuck out his jaw. Val, impressed, waited to hear what he had to say. It wasn't what she expected.

"Val is *not* my girlfriend! You take that back!'' Toby blustered.

Val put a hand on his arm. "Take it easy, Toby. Let me handle this,'' she murmured. Turning to Mr. Wetzel, she said, trying to control her temper, "Mr. Wetzel, my father didn't steal Pedro. He took him to Animal Inn because Pedro was sick and you'd mistreated him. And Miss Maggie Rafferty paid you five hundred dollars for him at the county fair. So nobody stole anything from you. Now do you have a bicycle pump we could borrow so we can go home?''

"I ain't got no bicycle pump, 'cause I ain't got

no bicycle," Wetzel growled. "I ain't got nothin' for you kids. So like I said, you better make tracks 'fore I sic Champ on you!"

Toby had sidled around to the back of the truck, and now he said, "Hey, Mr. Wetzel, how come you bought all those bags of cat and dog food? I guess you have a lot of pets, huh? We heard some dogs barking a little while ago."

Wetzel glared at him and his mean little eyes looked even meaner and smaller. "It ain't none of your business how many pets I have! Now get movin'! And don't come back, neither!"

Val and Toby looked at each other.

"Okay, Mr. Wetzel. We're going," Toby said.

They started walking toward the barn to fetch their bikes.

"We're going, all right," Val muttered to Toby. "But we'll be back, that's for sure! He's hiding some animals in that shed, and I bet a whole week's salary that they're the same ones that are missing!"

Toby nodded grimly. "Me, too. But we still don't have proof." Then he brightened. "Hey Val, what if we snuck out here late at night and broke into the shed? Then we'd know for sure! And we could tell the sheriff, and he'd come out here with his deputy and throw old Wetzel in the slammer, and we'd be heroes!"

They began wheeling their bikes back down the

lane to the main road, glancing behind them every few steps to make sure Mr. Wetzel's nasty old dog wasn't coming after them.

"We can't do that, Toby," Val said. "That'd be breaking and entering, and that's as illegal as what Mr. Wetzel is doing — *if* he's doing it. Besides, I don't want to be a hero. All I want is to get those animals back to their owners."

"So how are we going to do it then?" Toby asked. "Got any brilliant ideas?"

"No," Val admitted. "But I think it's time we talked to Dad. I didn't tell him we were coming out here today, and he doesn't know that we think Mr. Wetzel is involved. Why don't you eat supper at my house tonight? We can tell him everything then, and I bet he'll have some good ideas."

"Okay, I'll·call my folks when we get to your house — if we ever do." Toby looked down the road that led to Essex. "It's gonna be a real long walk!"

Chapter
7

It turned out not to be as long a walk as Val and Toby had feared, because, before they had gone very far, they heard the brisk clip-clop of hooves on the road behind them. Turning, they saw Miss Maggie driving her cart. Pedro didn't look any sadder than the last time Val had seen him, but he didn't look any happier, either. As for Miss Maggie, her bright blue eyes peered out from under the wide brim of what once must have been a very elegant straw hat. Its faded ribbons and wilted flowers made a startling contrast to her usual costume of baggy pants and khaki shirt. Anyone else would have looked ridiculous in such an outfit, but somehow Miss Maggie didn't look ridiculous at all.

"Hi there, Val Taylor and Toby Curran," she sang out. "Looks like you could use a lift. I've got a bicycle pump somewhere at home. Hop in and we'll fix that flat."

"Gee thanks, Miss Maggie," Toby said. He lifted his bike and Val's into the back of the cart, then climbed in while Val got up on the seat next to her.

Miss Maggie clucked at Pedro, and the burro started plodding along again.

"What're you two doing out in this neck of the woods?" Miss Maggie asked.

"Visiting Mr. Wetzel's farm," Val told her. "You see, Miss Maggie, it's like this . . ."

By the time she had finished telling their suspicions about the gang of petnappers, Wetzel's possible connection with them, and what had happened at the farm, Miss Maggie's weathered face was set in a grim scowl.

"That's just the kind of thing John Wetzel would do!" she muttered. "Mean and evil clear through, that's what he is. Always was, even when he was a little tyke. I ought to know — I was his third-grade teacher 'way back before either of you were even thought of." She glanced at Val. "What does young Theodore have to say about all this?"

"We haven't told Dad yet," Val said. "But we're going to tonight as soon as he gets back from Harrisburg."

Miss Maggie nodded, and the roses and ribbons on her astonishing hat bobbed and quivered. "Young Theodore has a good head on his shoulders. Always did. I was *his* third-grade teacher, too, you know."

"My dad was in your class, too, when he was a kid," Toby called from the back of the cart. "He says you were one of the best teachers he ever had."

70

Miss Maggie's head snapped around. "*One* of the best?"

"*The* best," Toby quickly said. "The very best!"

Miss Maggie sniffed. "I should certainly hope so!" She tugged gently on the reins, and Pedro turned down Mount Holly Lane, heading toward Maggie's enormous old house.

"After you fix that tire, Toby Curran," Miss Maggie called over her shoulder, "you and Val and I are going to have some lemonade and cookies, and we're going to talk about how to fix John Wetzel once and for all. The lemonade's frozen, and the cookies are store-bought, but I guarantee that you'll find my suggestions very original!"

Val didn't doubt it in the least.

Half an hour later, Val, Toby, and Miss Maggie were seated in the sunporch of Miss Maggie's house. Val and Toby sat on an ancient wicker settee whose flowered cushions had seen better days, and Miss Maggie sat in an equally antique matching wicker chair. The lemonade, frozen or not, tasted delicious, and the cookies, though they weren't nearly as good as Mrs. Racer's, weren't all that bad.

The only problem was that all the stray dogs Miss Maggie had adopted from the Humane Society Shelter kept trying to snatch the cookies from the plate, and sometimes even from their hands. Her cats — there must have been at least a dozen of them, Val thought — weren't nearly as badly behaved. They just hid under the furniture or lolled on top of it or leaped into everyone's lap, purring loudly. Between the yapping of the dogs and the purring of the cats, it was a little hard to hear what Miss Maggie was saying.

"What I suggest is this," Miss Maggie yelled, lifting a black-and-white cat from her lap and plopping it onto the floor. "If there really *is* such a gang as you describe, and if John Wetzel is the mastermind behind it — though considering what I know of John Wetzel's mind, it seems highly unlikely — what we have to do is catch him in the act . . . *down*, Rupert!" She tapped the nose of a short-haired yellow mutt that had just made a lunge for one of the remaining cookies. "No manners," she sighed. "No manners at all. As I was saying, we have to catch them in the act of stealing an animal. And as you suggest, tonight would seem to be the time when this hypothetical gang might strike again."

"Uh . . . Miss Maggie?" Toby raised his hand, as though he were one of the students in her third-grade class.

"Yes?"

"What does 'hypothetical' mean?"

"It means," Miss Maggie said, "supposed or assumed. In other words, guesswork. Don't they teach you anything in school nowadays? To return to the topic at hand. . . . Melisande, leave Hamlet alone! He didn't mean to bite your tail. . . . Where was I? Oh, yes. The petnappers. What we need is a decoy. You *do* know what a decoy is, don't you?"

Toby and Val both nodded.

"Good! This decoy must be an animal that appears to be alone, unsupervised, and up for grabs. Preferably a dog, I think." She scanned the roomful of animals with her bright blue gaze. "Let's see . . . Rupert would do, or perhaps Juliet."

A perky little spaniel raised her head at the sound of her name and wagged her stubby tail.

"Now here's my plan," Miss Maggie went on. "As soon as it gets dark, I'll let Juliet — or Rupert — out into my yard. And if those ruffians arrive, I will immediately call the sheriff. Since it will undoubtedly take Sheriff Weigel so long to get here that the petnappers will make a clean getaway, I'll simply follow them on my bike."

Val and Toby looked at each other.

"Gee, Miss Maggie," Val said, "that's a really interesting idea, but . . ."

"But what?" Miss Maggie snapped. "I suppose you think I'm too old to go kiting around on a bicycle in the middle of the night, don't you?"

"Well . . ." That was exactly what Val had been thinking, but she didn't want to say so.

"What Val means is that it's a great idea, but it probably won't work," Toby said bluntly. Unfazed by Miss Maggie's frown, he added, "It won't work because I don't think the petnappers will come to your house again. They've already been here once, when they got Ludwig, so they'd know you'd be on the lookout for them."

Miss Maggie nodded. "Good point, Toby. That hadn't occurred to me. Well then, I'll just bring Juliet — or Rupert — to the Taylors' house. I'm sure young Theodore won't mind when I explain the situation to him. Yes, that's a much better idea, now that I think about it." She stood up and dusted cookie crumbs off her pants. "Now that everything's settled, you two run along. Toby, I suggest you ask your father if you can come over to the Taylors' tonight — we might need an extra pair of hands. Tell young Theodore that I'll be there around eight-thirty, Val. And of course, if he comes up with a better plan of action, I will be more than happy to listen to it. Try not to let any of the cats out when you go." Bending down and hooking one bony finger through the collar of a large, furry gray-and-white dog, she said, "Come, Robinson Crusoe. Time for your bath!"

Val and Toby followed Miss Maggie and a reluctant Robinson Crusoe out of the sunporch, with assorted cats and dogs frisking around their feet.

"Thanks for the lemonade and cookies," Val called after her as she clumped through the big, dim living room and down an even dimmer hallway.

"Don't mention it," Miss Maggie called over her

74

shoulder. "And don't worry — Ludwig and the other pets are as good as found!"

Edging out the front door and closing it quickly behind them so no cats could escape, Val and Toby crossed the wide front porch and ran down the steps to where their bikes were parked.

"That old lady is something else!" Toby said as he wheeled his bike down the path to the gate. "Is she always like that?"

Val nodded, grinning. "Always. When Miss Maggie makes up her mind to do something, she does it. But I can't help wondering what Dad's going to think about this plan of hers."

When they reached Val's house, they found Mrs. Racer in the kitchen making watermelon pickles. As she took the last jar out of a pot of boiling water with a pair of tongs, she said, "Oh, Vallie, there you are. Hello, Toby. Find any of them missing animals?"

"Not yet," Val told her, "but we think we have some clues about where they are." Picking up Cleveland while Toby patted Jocko and Sunshine, she asked, "Are Teddy and Erin home yet?"

"Nope, and they won't be, neither, not till tomorrow morning. Teddy's sleeping over at Eric's tonight — Eric's mom called to ask if it was all right and I said it was. And Erin's sleeping over at Olivia's. I talked to Olivia's mom, too. So it'll be just you and Doc for supper tonight — unless Toby's staying. You staying, Toby?"

"If it's okay with my folks. Can I use the phone to call my mom?" Toby asked.

"Sure," Val said. "And don't forget to ask if you can hang out for a while, like Miss Maggie said. Maybe you ought to ask if you can sleep over, just in case the petnappers don't show up until real late."

"Sleep over?" Toby squawked. "At a *girl's* house? Gimme a break, Val! My brothers would laugh themselves sick. I'll say . . ." he thought for a minute. "I'll ask Mom if I can have supper here, and then I'll tell her that Miss Maggie asked me to spend the night at her house because she's scared the petnappers might come back. Yeah, that's what I'll say."

"Miss Maggie? Scared?" Val echoed.

"Well, a *normal* old lady would be," Toby pointed out. "And if Miss Maggie was a normal old lady, she'd want a man around the house for protection."

It was hard for Val not to smile at Toby calling himself a man, but she managed to keep a straight face. "Just call, okay?"

After Toby had called and gotten permission from his mother, he and Val went into the living room, turned on the fan, and settled down to watch TV. They became so wrapped up in a program about endangered species in Africa that they didn't notice the passage of time. The honking of a car horn outside took them by surprise.

"That's m'son Henry," Mrs. Racer said, hurrying

out of the kitchen. "Vallie, I made two kinds of chili, with meat and without. And there's a green salad in the icebox. All you have to do is pour on some of that store-bought dressing." She paused and looked at the clock on the mantel. "I wonder where Doc is? It's past six — he should've been back from Harrisburg before now. Maybe I ought to stay . . ."

"Mrs. Racer, we'll be fine," Val assured her. "Dad will be home any minute now, and Henry's waiting for you. See you tomorrow, okay?"

"Well, I guess. . . . Don't answer the door unless it's somebody you know, and don't burn the chili if you can help it."

"Maybe I'd better heat up the chili," Toby said with a grin as Mrs. Racer bustled out. "I remember Teddy said once that he bet you could figure out a way to burn water!"

Val was about to throw a sofa pillow at him when the phone rang, so she settled for punching him in the arm instead as she dashed to answer it.

"Vallie? It's Dad. Listen, honey, I've got a problem," her father said. "I'm not going to make it home for supper. In fact, I might not make it home at all tonight — the car conked out on me, and it's sitting in a garage here in Harrisburg. My friends, the Harveys, have offered to put me up for the night if the mechanic can't finish the repairs until tomorrow."

"Oh, no — the poor old car!" Val sighed. The Taylors' car was twelve years old, and bit by bit it was falling apart. But Doc hadn't wanted to take the van today in case Mike needed it to pick up a sick or injured animal. "And poor you. Don't worry about us, Dad. Teddy and Erin are sleeping over at their friends' houses, and Toby and Miss Maggie are going to be here tonight."

"Miss Maggie? Why in the world . . ." There was a clicking noise, and Doc said, "Drat! My three minutes can't be up yet. Why is Miss Maggie . . ." The clicking noise continued. "Honey, there's something wrong with this phone. I'm glad you won't be alone in the house. See you later tonight, I hope, and then you can tell me why — " The phone went dead.

Val hung up the receiver and went back into the living room. "That was Dad," she told Toby. "The car broke down and he might not be able to get home tonight. And then the phone got peculiar so I couldn't tell him about Miss Maggie's idea."

"Well, that means it's up to you and me to catch the petnappers," Toby said cheerfully.

"And Miss Maggie," Val reminded him.

After supper, Toby decided to go for a bike ride while Val called Jill to tell her about the trip to Mr. Wetzel's farm, their visit with Miss Maggie, and what they were planning to do that night.

"Oh, Val, that sounds really exciting!" Jill cried. "I wish I could come over, too, but I'm baby-sitting tonight. Let me know what happens first thing to-morrow, will you? It would be so wonderful if you got Patches back for me!"

"I'll call you before I go to work," Val promised. "Now I have to go — I have to feed the rabbits, the chickens, and the duck, and walk Jocko and Sunshine since Teddy and Erin aren't here. Talk to you tomorrow."

"And Val, be careful, okay?" Jill said. "I mean, those guys probably won't come, but if they do, I wouldn't want you to get hurt, or Toby or Miss Maggie, either."

"I'll be careful," Val assured her. "Believe it or not, I was so careful tonight that I didn't even burn the chili!"

Chapter
8

Promptly at eight-thirty, there was a loud knock at the kitchen door. Val and Toby had just come back from walking the dogs, and Val let Miss Maggie in. As she patted Jocko and Sunshine, Miss Maggie said, "I decided on Juliet."

Val and Toby stared at her, confused for a moment. Then Toby said, "Oh, you mean instead of Rupert."

"Of course. I don't suppose you thought I was intending to play the balcony scene from Shakespeare's play, did you?" Miss Maggie said with a grin. "I have to admit I'm a little long in the tooth for that role. Yes, I brought Juliet, only because she's smaller and fit in the basket of my bike. Rupert is more sensible, but he's too big." She glanced at Val "I guess you're wondering why I didn't suggest we use either Jocko or Sunshine for our decoy, aren't you?" Before Val could reply, she went on, "Because Jocko's too scatterbrained and Sunshine's too old. Now about this gang . . ."

"This *hypothetical* gang," Toby put in proudly.

Miss Maggie nodded in approval. "Very good, Toby. Learn a new word every day and by the time you're as old as I am, you'll be a walking dictionary. As I was saying, this hypothetical gang will probably not show up. But if they do, we will be ready for them. Val, where is your father? I assume you've told him what we have in mind."

"Dad's stuck in Harrisburg," Val said. "His car broke down. I tried to tell him but something was the matter with the phone when he called. Uh . . . Miss Maggie, exactly what *do* we have in mind? And where's Juliet?"

"I tied Juliet to the apple tree out back. As for what we have in mind, I've altered my initial plan somewhat. Chasing after the thieves on my bicycle is probably impractical. So I've brought this along." She held up a battery-powered lantern. "If Juliet is attacked, I will be on your back porch, and I'll turn on my flashlight. You and Toby will be concealed in that treehouse next to the garage, watching closely. You'll be able to see the thief — or thieves — very clearly and so will I. Between the three of us, we'll have an accurate description of the person or persons involved, which we will then relay to Sheriff Weigel by telephone. From then on, it's up to him."

"You mean all we're going to do is *look*?" Toby said, disappointed. "We're not going to tackle 'em or anything?"

"Absolutely not!" Miss Maggie scowled. "No heroics, Toby — or you either, Val. We watch, and we report. Is that clear?"

Val nodded, and Toby said, "Yeah, if you say so."

"I say so." Miss Maggie looked out the kitchen window. "It's almost dark now. I suggest we take up our positions and wait."

"Sounds pretty dull to me," Toby muttered to Val as she turned off the light and followed Miss Maggie outside.

"I don't think it sounds dull at all," Val told him. "We're going to be spies up in Teddy's treehouse, watching out for the petnappers. That's really exciting!"

"Yeah — exciting."

Miss Maggie took up her position on the back porch while Val and Toby crossed the lawn and climbed up the old apple tree. "Watch out for the third board in the floor," Val whispered. "It's kind of rotten — you don't want to fall through. Dad's been meaning to replace it for ages, but Teddy hardly ever comes up here anymore. This treehouse is pretty old, you know. Dad built it for me when I was a little kid."

"Hey, this is neat!" Toby said, settling down next to the trunk. He looked up at the roof. "You can see lots of stars through the holes."

Val smiled. "I know. Those holes are supposed

to be there. I used to sleep out here in the summer sometimes, and I'd look at the stars for hours and hours." She flopped down on her back, folding her arms under her head.

"I'm going to watch them all night long," Toby said. "I'm never going to go to sleep."

"Neither am I . . ."

They were jolted awake by the sound of a police siren — *Wowowowowow!*

"It's the cops!" Toby yelled. "They've come to catch the gang!" He leaped to his feet, and so did Val. Through sleep-dimmed eyes, they looked down and saw the backyard flooded with light. Right beneath them, somebody was struggling with a small, yapping bundle of fur.

"They've got Juliet!" Val screamed. "Toby, we've got to *do* something! We've got to see his face!"

"I'm looking! I'm . . . *looooooking!*"

Suddenly Toby disappeared from sight. The floor had given way beneath him, and he landed on top of the person below.

"*Oof!*" the person grunted. Juliet leaped out of his arms and dashed to Miss Maggie, who was standing on the porch, holding her powerful flashlight and *wowowowing* at the top of her lungs. She stopped though, when she picked up the little dog.

As Val scrambled down the ladder, she heard

the sound of an engine revving up followed by a loud crunch of metal meeting metal.

"What's going on here? Hey, you — where do you think you're going?"

Val couldn't believe her ears. It was Dad! He'd come home, and he was grappling in the driveway with someone! She looked around wildly and picked up the first thing she saw — an empty flower pot. Charging into the driveway where Doc and the stranger were struggling, she raised the flower pot over her head with both hands and brought it down on the stranger's head. The man let out a grunt of pain and surprise as he dropped to the ground and sat there clutching his head and moaning.

"Dad, are you okay?" Val cried. She couldn't see much of anything because the driveway was very dark in contrast to the brightly lighted yard. Suddenly she had an awful thought. What if it was her father she'd hit instead of the prowler?

"I'm just fine, honey," Doc said. "Thanks for the assistance. Now tell me what's happening? I was pulling into the driveway when a car rammed into me. Then this joker jumped out and started running, so I tackled him." He peered down into Val's face in the dim light. "Are *you* all right?"

"Oh yes, I'm fine, Dad. And so are Toby and Miss Maggie. But those petnappers aren't!"

"Petnappers?" Doc echoed.

"Yes! I kept trying to tell you, but . . ."

"*Ooooh!*" groaned the man who was sitting in the driveway. Now that Val's eyes were accustomed to the dim light, she saw that he wasn't a man at all. He was a teenager and he looked scared.

Doc bent down and grabbed one of the boy's arms. "Come on, fellow," he said grimly. "I think you owe us an explanation."

The boy staggered to his feet and allowed himself to be led into the backyard. Miss Maggie had put her lantern down on the top step of the porch. Still holding the quivering spaniel, she was standing over Toby and his captive, another teenaged boy. As Val, Doc, and their prisoner came into the yard, the boy Toby was sitting on managed to raise his head from the grass.

"Steve!" Toby gasped. "What're *you* doing here? Ralph told me . . ."

Steve spat grass and dirt out of his mouth so he could talk. "I know what Ralph told you. He told you what I told *him*! I didn't want my kid brother to know what I was doing." He looked up at the boy whose arm Doc was still holding. "Hey, Skeeter," he said weakly. "What's happening?"

"That's a dumb thing to ask!" Skeeter said. "Same thing that's happening to you. These guys nailed us . . ." He glanced over at Val. "These guys and this *girl*. You've got some arm, you know that?" he said to Val.

Val smiled sweetly at him. "I'm on the Hamilton

85

Raiders softball team. And my dad taught me everything I know." Then the name registered. *"Skeeter?*
You're the chief petnapper! Hey, Dad, we caught
the leader of the gang!"

"Exactly as I anticipated." Miss Maggie grinned
at Doc. "My plan worked out precisely the way I
had intended it to. But I have to admit your arrival,
though unexpected, was a great help. And now I
think it's time we called the sheriff."

Doc nodded. "I think maybe you're right."

"Naturally," said Miss Maggie.

While they were waiting for Sheriff Weigel to
arrive, Doc, Val, Miss Maggie, Toby, and the petnappers went into the house and sat down in the
living room. According to the clock on the fireplace
mantel, it was half-past two in the morning.

"Suppose you fill me in on the details," Doc
said, wearily rubbing his eyes. "Skeeter — that's not
your real name, is it? How did you get involved in
this?"

Skeeter slumped on the couch, staring down at
the floor. "Melrose," he muttered. "That's my real
name. *Melrose!* Can you believe it? I've been trying
to live that name down all my life! But that's not
important."

"No, it certainly is not," Miss Maggie snapped.
"Keep talking."

"Well, it's like this. I was short of cash — I'm

always short of cash — and this old guy came up to me one day and told me I could make a lot of bucks if I'd bring him some animals. He said he could sell them, and he'd pay me fifty percent of what he got . . ."

"From the Spring Valley lab?" Val asked eagerly.

"Yeah, from them, and from other places, like pet shops and stuff. This old guy . . ."

"Mr. Wetzel?" Toby asked.

"Yeah — him. Big bucks, he said. He said he could sell anything with four legs and a tail to Spring Valley. And if me and my gang could snatch some pedigreed pets, like Mrs. Van Fleet's cat, he could sell *them* to a pet dealer in Philadelphia who didn't ask questions."

"John Wetzel, eh? Somehow that doesn't surprise me," Doc said grimly. "So, Melrose," (Skeeter cringed) "have you made a lot of money on this deal?"

Melrose/Skeeter shook his head. "Not a dime, have we, Steve?"

"Nope. And here I was hoping to make enough to buy that motorcycle I've been wanting. John Wetzel's a crook, that's what he is," Steve said.

"So what does that make *you*?" Toby asked, scowling at his friend's brother.

Steve didn't answer.

"Are the stolen animals at Mr. Wetzel's farm?" Val asked.

Skeeter nodded. "He's waiting ten days, then he'll deliver them to the lab and to the pet dealer. He keeps saying we'll get our money when he does, but I don't believe him." He looked at Doc and asked in a small voice, "What's going to happen to us? Will we go to jail?"

Doc looked at him levelly. "Not if you take us to Wetzel's farm and release the stolen animals so we can return them to their owners."

Miss Maggie cackled with glee. "But John Wetzel's going to go to jail, that's for sure! And it serves him right. If it weren't such a cliché, I'd say I hope they lock him up and throw away the key!"

The ringing of the doorbell made everybody jump.

"That must be Sheriff Weigel," Val said, running to answer the door. "Let's take him out to Mr. Wetzel's farm right now!"

Chapter
9

Sheriff Weigel, wearing his uniform pants and jacket over his striped pajamas, was hustled out the door almost before he came in. Doc explained what had happened as he escorted Steve and Skeeter to the sheriff's car and handed them over to a yawning deputy. Miss Maggie, still holding Juliet, climbed into the front seat beside Sheriff Weigel.

"Do you have a search warrant with you, Buddy?" she asked.

" 'Buddy?' " Toby whispered to Val. "I thought the sheriff's name was William."

Val giggled. "It is. But what do you bet he was in her third-grade class, and that's what he was called when he was a little boy?"

"No bet," Toby said, grinning.

"Yes, Miss Maggie, I've got one right here, somewhere," the sheriff said. "Maybe in the glove compartment . . ."

"Good! Then we're all set." Miss Maggie settled Juliet more comfortably in her lap. "Drive on!"

"Hey, wait a minute!" Doc said, sticking his

head in the car window. "Val, Toby, and I captured these boys . . ."

"The perpetrators," Sheriff Weigel corrected.

"Right. Anyway, hang on while I see if I can start my car and we'll drive to Wetzel's farm with you. Melrose backed into me when he was trying to escape, but with any luck, the engine wasn't damaged."

"Melrose? Who's Melrose?" the sheriff asked.

"*Skeeter!*" Melrose/Skeeter yelled.

Doc, Val, and Toby piled into Doc's car, and to their surprise and relief it started immediately. Doc backed out of the driveway and followed the sheriff's car down the dark, silent streets of Essex.

"What if old man Wetzel comes after us with a shotgun?" Toby asked nervously. "Or sics his mean old dog on us?"

"He'd hardly risk shooting the sheriff," Doc said. In the faint light from the dashboard, Val could see his mouth curving in a smile. "And if he sics Champ on us, we'll sic Miss Maggie on *him*!"

Mr. Wetzel's decrepit farm was in total darkness as the two cars turned into the muddy, rutted lane that led to the barn and the other ramshackle buildings. Sheriff Weigel stopped his car by the barnyard, and Doc pulled up next to him. Miss Maggie got out and plopped Juliet on the seat.

"Sit and stay!" she said firmly. Then she began striding toward the farmhouse.

"Here! Miss Maggie, where are you going? Wait for me!" Sheriff Weigel called, stumbling after her. "I'm the sheriff, you know!"

Val heard Miss Maggie shout back, "You may be the sheriff, William Weigel, but you'll always be Buddy to me!"

She stamped up the rickety steps to Mr. Wetzel's porch and banged on the front door.

"John Wetzel, open this door immediately!"

Sheriff Weigel joined her and hollered, "Open up in the name of the law!"

Loud barks and growls came from inside, but no lights went on and nobody appeared.

"Maybe he's left town," Steve said hopefully. Neither he nor Skeeter were looking forward to Wetzel's reaction when he saw that they'd shown up with the police instead of with more stolen pets.

"Yeah, that's it — he's left town. Let's come back tomorrow, okay?" Skeeter took a step in the direction of the sheriff's car, but Doc grabbed his arm and the deputy held Steve.

"I suggest you both stay right where you are," Doc said.

Val and Toby went up on the porch. "Hey, Sheriff," Toby whispered excitedly, "why don't you yell 'Come out with your hands up! We've got the place surrounded!' That's what they do in the movies."

Miss Maggie glared at him. "Toby Curran, this is *not* the movies. Control yourself!"

Just then the door to the farmhouse flew open and John Wetzel appeared in the doorway, holding Champ by the collar. Champ's yellow fangs were bared, and so were Mr. Wetzel's yellow teeth. They both looked so fierce that Val stepped back a pace, right onto Toby's foot.

"Sorry," she whispered when he let out a muffled squawk.

Wetzel's small, evil eyes squinted at Miss Maggie in the dim light from the hallway behind him. "Are you crazy, old woman?" he shouted. "You got no call t' come bangin' on decent people's doors in the middle of the night! Now scat, 'fore I call the cops!"

Miss Maggie smirked. "Too late, John Wetzel. They're here." She stepped aside, revealing the sheriff right behind her.

Wetzel gawked at Sheriff Weigel, open-mouthed. Then he said weakly, "Well, if it ain't Buddy Weigel. Long time no see, Buddy. Somethin' I can do for you?"

"Matter of fact, there is," the sheriff said mildly. "I got a couple of boys here who say you have some animals that don't belong to you. So I'd appreciate it if you'd let me and these other folks here take a look around your place, kind of check it out if you know what I mean." As Wetzel started to object, Sheriff Weigel added, "In case you're interested, John, I got a search warrant, so everything's nice and legal. You want to lead the tour?"

"If you'd rather we made the search ourselves, that's okay too," Val said. "Toby and I have a pretty good idea of where to start."

Wetzel scowled at Val and Toby. "You two again! What're you kids doin' here at this time o' night? I bet your folks'd be real mad if they knew what you were up to!" he blustered.

"*I* know," Doc called out from where he stood with the deputy, Skeeter, and Steve. "Make it easy on yourself, Wetzel. If you cooperate, maybe you won't spend more than a few months in jail. Otherwise . . ."

Wetzel seemed to shrivel right before their eyes. "I'm a poor man, Buddy," he whined, and Champ began to whine, too. "A poor man's gotta make a livin' the best he can, right? Ain't that the American way? So when I seen an opportunity, I took it. This here's the land of opportunity, ain't it? You're not gonna haul me in, are you, Buddy? We were in third grade together — in this here fine woman's class . . ." He bared his yellow teeth at Miss Maggie in what Val supposed was an attempt at a smile.

"John Wetzel, you are a disgrace to the Pennsylvania school system," Miss Maggie barked, "and an insult to my third-grade class!"

Val and Toby hurried off the porch in the direction of the shed from which they had heard the barking earlier that day. As they ran, they heard Sheriff Weigel say, "You had your chance, John, and you blew it. And another thing — *don't call me Buddy!*"

As Val had expected, they found all the missing animals in Mr. Wetzel's shed. The minute she and Toby opened the door, they were greeted with happy barks and yelps as all the dogs danced around them, wagging their tails and leaping up to lick their faces. Ludwig almost knocked Val down when he dashed out the door, making a beeline for Miss Maggie. The old lady gave him such a big hug that Ludwig let out a strangled *"woof!"* Val was sure she saw tears in Miss Maggie's bright blue eyes, though all she said was, "Well, Ludwig. Nice to have you back again. Pedro will be very pleased."

The cats were in another tumbledown building not far from the shed where Mr. Wetzel had hidden the dogs. Val spotted Patches immediately. The kitten's parti-colored fur made her stand out from the other cats, and her raspy *"meow"* was very familiar to Val. She picked Patches up and cuddled her in her arms. If there had been a phone anywhere near, Val would have called Jill even though it was now three-thirty, and the earliest earlybirds were already drowsily chirping.

By the light of Miss Maggie's lantern, Doc

quickly examined Ludwig, Patches and several of the other animals. Much to Val's relief, he found them all in good health and well-fed.

"Well, o' course they're well-fed," Wetzel whined. "Them animals been eatin' more than I have!" He turned to Toby. "You seen all that pet food I bought today. Best quality, too." Now he appealed to Sheriff Weigel. "That there pet food cost me a bundle, Bud — uh — Sheriff. You ask Chuck Shorb over at White Rose Feed if it didn't. Yessir, I been takin' mighty good care o' these cats and dogs, ain't I, boys?" he asked Skeeter and Steve.

Steve nodded. "Yeah, but only because Skeeter and me told you they wouldn't be worth a plugged nickel if they weren't in good shape when you tried to sell 'em," he mumbled.

"You should've seen these two sheds before Steve and me cleaned 'em out," Skeeter said to Doc and the sheriff.

"I can well imagine," Doc replied dryly. "Well, Sheriff, what do we do now?"

Sheriff Weigel rubbed his chin. "Not much we *can* do about getting all these animals back to their rightful owners at this hour . . ."

"Needless to say, I'm taking Ludwig home with me," Miss Maggie put in.

"And I'll take Patches," Val offered. "I'll deliver her to Jill first thing tomorrow morning. I mean, *this* morning."

"Guess it won't hurt the rest of them to stay here a while longer," the sheriff said. "You say none of them need medical attention, Doc?" Doc nodded. "Well, then, here's what we'll do. Frank, you and I will take Steve and Melrose home to their parents, and we'll drop Wetzel off at the county jail on the way."

"Gotcha, sheriff," the deputy said. Wetzel, Skeeter, and Steve all groaned.

Sheriff Weigel turned to the two boys. "I'm gonna tell your folks exactly what you've been up to. I don't guess they'll be real happy about it, do you?"

"My dad'll probably skin me alive," Skeeter muttered.

"Mine, too," Steve agreed.

"Skin or no skin, I'll expect you both to show up at my office tomorrow at noon on the dot," the sheriff went on. "And I want you to bring the other members of the gang with you, understand? How many are there, anyway?"

"Only three," Skeeter said. "But they didn't come out tonight."

"You just see that they come out at noon. If they don't, I'll hold you and your pal here personally responsibile."

"What . . . what're you gonna do with us?" Steve quavered.

Sheriff Weigel sighed. "Blamed if I know! I'm too tired to think straight."

"May I make a suggestion?" Doc asked.

"Sure — be my guest."

"Well, I'm a firm believer in making the punishment fit the crime," Doc said. "I suggest that Skeeter, Steve, and their accomplices be made to return each and every animal to its owner — under your supervision, of course — and apologize to every man, woman, and child for stealing their pets. And I further suggest that after they've done so, all five of them be required to perform forty hours each of community service by working at the Humane Society Shelter, caring for lost and abandoned animals."

"Excellent suggestions, both of them," Miss Maggie said. "As I told your daughter, you always did have a good head on your shoulders, Theodore!"

"Sounds good to me," Sheriff Weigel agreed wearily. "Okay, everybody, let's hit the road. If we're lucky we might just manage to get to bed before dawn."

Val hadn't realized until that very minute how tired she was. She could hardly keep her eyes open as she stumbled along beside Doc to their car. Patches, she noticed, was sound asleep in her arms.

Toby's eyelids were drooping, too, but Miss Maggie and Ludwig were so glad to be reunited that they couldn't have been more wide awake. Val's last thought before she dozed off in the front seat was of how happy all the missing animals' owners would be when their beloved pets were returned. Jill, and Sparky, and Rose, and Mrs. Van Fleet, and Mr. Corcoran, and. . . .

Chapter
10

For the first time since Val could remember, neither her internal alarm clock nor her family woke up in time for work. It was almost eleven o'clock when she finally opened her eyes to see Patches curled up on the pillow next to her head and Cleveland sitting next to her feet. Cleveland didn't look very happy about the kitten. When Val sat up and gathered all twelve pounds of orange cat into her arms, he peered over her shoulder and hissed at Patches.

Val laughed. "It's okay, Cleveland," she said, stroking him. "I'm taking Patches back to Jill right after breakfast. But first I need to shower and get dressed." She patted Patches, who was still sound asleep. "I guess Dad must have gone to Animal Inn without me. Wonder where Toby is?" Val dimly remembered Doc taking Toby to Teddy's room last night. She had glanced in on her way to her own room and saw Toby sprawled across Teddy's bed, fully dressed and sound asleep.

In the bathroom she found a note taped to the

mirror over the basin. "Hi, sleepyhead," she read. "I walked the dogs. Doc and I are going to work. Doc says come out after you take Patches home. We told Mrs. Racer about last night. Sincerely yours, Toby."

Her question answered, Val quickly showered and put on shorts and her favorite "Save the Whales" T-shirt. Then she hurried downstairs, carrying Patches. A very jealous Cleveland followed. After greeting the dogs and saying good morning to Mrs. Racer, she called Jill. The minute Jill heard her voice she said, "You found her! You found Patches! Oh, Val, I'm so happy! I'm coming right over!" She hung up before Val could say another word.

"How on earth did she know?" Val wondered aloud. "Unless Toby called her . . ."

"He didn't have to," Mrs. Racer said. "The whole town knows what you, Doc, and Toby did last night. Look here!" Beaming, she thrust the *Essex Gazette* under Val's nose.

"Special Late Edition" was printed in red across the top of the front page, and a banner headline proclaimed:

PETNAPPING RING BROKEN!

In smaller type, Val read, "Stolen Animals Found in Daring Midnight Raid on Wetzel Farm!" There was a picture of Mr. Wetzel, looking meaner than ever, standing between Sheriff Weigel and his deputy. Both the sheriff and Frank looked very proud of themselves. The caption beneath the picture read:

John Wetzel, 64, of Arbor Road (center) was apprehended in the early hours this morning by Sheriff William 'Buddy' Weigel (left) and Deputy Sheriff Frank Miller (right).

"Oh, wow!" breathed Val.

"Them reporter fellas sure were johnny-on-the-spot," Mrs. Racer said. "Read the article, Vallie! It tells how you and Miss Maggie Rafferty and Toby caught those kids who were stealing people's pets, and how Doc called the sheriff, and how you all went out to John Wetzel's farm, and . . ." She broke off, smiling. "I guess I just better let you read it for yourself."

Val put Patches down on the counter and read every word. Sheriff Weigel gave all the credit for solving the mystery of the missing animals to veterinarian Dr. Theodore Taylor, his daughter Valentine, Tobias Curran, and Miss Margaret Rafferty. He praised them for their quick thinking and prompt action in calling the sheriff's office, and announced that the stolen pets would be returned to their owners that very day.

John Wetzel, described as the mastermind of the petnapping gang, had rendered a full confession, and was being held in the county jail. Two of the young thieves, whose names had been withheld because of their ages, had confessed their part in the scheme as well, and had been remanded into the custody of their parents.

The article ended by quoting Sheriff Wetzel:

"Thanks to Doc Taylor, his daughter, and their friends, and Deputy Miller, and me, the citizens of Essex can rest easy once again, knowing that law and order have been restored to our fair town."

"Wow!" Val said again as she finished reading. "I wonder if Toby's seen this? He wanted to be a hero and now he is!"

"And so are you, Vallie, and so's Doc and Miss Maggie." Mrs. Racer put a plate of hot French toast on the kitchen table and poured a tall glass of orange juice. "Now you sit right down here and eat. You must be well nigh starved after all those goings-on last night."

Val discovered that Mrs. Racer was right. She was as hungry as a bear. As she poured maple syrup over her French toast and began to eat, Mrs. Racer fed Cleveland and Patches, keeping up a steady stream of excited chatter.

"Doc said you hit one of them bad boys on the head with a flower pot. Serves him right, that's what I say! That Melrose Cryder's been gettin' into trouble ever since he started callin' himself Skeeter. Now I ask you, what kind of a name is that? But I'm real surprised and disappointed in Steve Kunkle. Fine folks, the Kunkles. I bet his pop tanned his hide good when the sheriff brought him home. Maybe working at the shelter will straighten him out, and those other boys, too. The Devil finds work for idle hands, and that's the truth . . ."

Suddenly the back door flew open and Jill burst into the kitchen. "Patches!" she cried, picking up the kitten from the countertop and holding her tight. "Are you all right? You *look* all right. Is she all right, Val? Hi, Mrs. Racer. Isn't it wonderful? I could hardly believe my eyes when I saw the paper this morning! I just knew you'd bring Patches home, Val. Did Miss Maggie get Ludwig back? It must have been terribly exciting, going out to that awful man's farm in the dead of night! Tell me *everything*!"

But before Val could say a word, she heard the front door slam, and Teddy's voice shouting, "Vallie? Where are you? I smell French toast!" Jocko and Sunshine dashed out to meet him, and the three of them appeared in the kitchen a moment later. Over the dogs' excited barking, Teddy yelled, "Vallie, are you and Dad and Toby and Miss Maggie going to split all those rewards? Hi, Jill! Mrs. Racer, can I have some French toast? I'm starvin' like Marvin! I called Sparky to tell her, but she already knew — her mom's driving her out to old man Wetzel's stinky farm to pick up Charlie right this minute! Did he put up a big fight when you got there? Old man Wetzel, I mean, not Charlie. Boy, it must've been neat!"

103

"Well, it was — " Val began, but she was interrupted by Erin's arrival.

"Oh, Vallie, I read all about it in the paper!" her sister cried, running over to give Val a hug. "I'm so proud of you and Daddy, and Toby and Miss Maggie! It's so wonderful that all those people are going to get their pets back. . . . Oh, Jill, you've got Patches! I'm so happy for you! Mrs. Racer, is there any more French toast? It smells delicious — Teddy, don't hog all the syrup! Vallie, was the gang stealing animals for the Spring Valley lab like you thought?"

"It doesn't look that way," Val said. She was surprised that she'd actually been allowed to finish a sentence. "Mr. Wetzel was just planning to sell them to anybody who had the money to pay for them. Skeeter and Steve said something about the lab and a crooked pet dealer in Philadelphia. I guess the police will follow up on it."

"Boy, I wish I'd been home last night," Teddy mumbled through a mouthful of French toast. "Then my name would be in the paper, too. I missed all the fun!"

Erin shivered. "I'm glad I *wasn't* here! I'd have been scared to death!"

"Me, too," Jill admitted. "I think you're awfully brave, Val."

Val felt her cheeks growing pink. "I'm not really. Besides, there wasn't anything dangerous about it. With the sheriff and his deputy and the rest of us, we had Mr. Wetzel and those boys outnumbered two to one.'' Glancing at the kitchen clock, she exclaimed, "Oh, dear! It's half-past twelve! Dad will be wondering where I am, and Toby's probably asleep on his feet. Gotta run!''

"But Val, you didn't tell us *everything*!'' Jill complained as Val headed for the door.

"Later,'' Val called over her shoulder. "Right now, I have to get to work!''

That evening after supper, the Taylors, Jill, Toby, Sparky, and Mrs. Sparks were all seated around the biggest table in Curran's Ice-Cream Parlor. Mrs. Sparks had insisted on treating everybody to banana splits in celebration of Charlie's safe return, and Val, Toby, and Doc had just finished giving a blow-by-blow description of everything that had happened the night before.

"I can't *believe* it!'' Jill giggled. "You actually crowned that Skeeter with a *flower pot*, Val?''

"Cool!'' Teddy added admiringly.

"Hey, don't forget that I jumped out of your treehouse right on top of Steve,'' Toby said. "He didn't know what hit him!''

"You didn't jump, you fell,'' Val pointed out. "Dad, you really have to fix that floor. There's an enormous hole now.''

"Well, I *would've* jumped if the board hadn't given way,'' Toby said.

"Who gets the reward money, Dad?" Teddy asked. "You haven't said anything about that. I think you and Vallie and Toby and Miss Maggie oughta get it, like I told Vallie this morning!"

"In the first place, Teddy, only Mrs. Van Fleet, Mr. Corcoran, and Mrs. Sparks were offering rewards," Doc told him. "And in the second place, we don't really need the money."

"But the Humane Society Shelter does," Mrs. Sparks added. "So I spoke to Mrs. Van Fleet and Mr. Corcoran today, and we all agreed to give the money to the society instead."

Doc smiled at her. "On behalf of the board of directors, I thank you very much!"

"That's terrific!" Val exclaimed.

"Oh, yes — one other thing," Doc said, grinning. "Remember all that cat and dog food Mr. Wetzel bought yesterday?"

Toby and Val nodded.

"Well, it seems he's agreed to donate it to the shelter, too."

"I bet I know whose idea that was!" Erin said. "Yours, right, Daddy?"

"I *did* happen to mention it to the sheriff this afternoon," Doc replied, his eyes twinkling.

"Dad, what about the Spring Valley lab people?" Val asked. "Were they involved in the petnapping scheme at all?"

Doc shook his head. "No, Vallie. Sheriff Weigel

checked with them. They knew nothing about it. They had never even heard of John Wetzel."

Sparky bounced up and down in her chair. "Where are our banana splits, Mom? We ordered them ages and *ages* ago!"

"Philomena, don't tell me you're dying of hunger," her mother sighed. "You ate an enormous supper less than an hour ago."

"I know, Mom." Sparky grinned. "But I have to make up for everything I didn't eat while Charlie was gone."

"I wonder where Miss Maggie is," Mrs. Sparks said. "I asked her to join us tonight."

Doc stood up. "Maybe I'd better give her a call . . ."

"Don't bother, Daddy," Erin said, peering out the plate glass window. "Here they come now!"

"They?" Val turned to look, and saw Pedro's cart coming into the parking lot. Pedro's ears were standing straight up, and Val could swear that if donkeys could smile, Pedro was smiling. Sitting next to Miss Maggie in his usual place was Ludwig, and he was smiling, too. So was Miss Maggie. She pulled Pedro to a stop next to the Animal Inn van, hopped out of the cart, and tied Pedro to the bumper. With Ludwig trotting happily at her side, she strode briskly to the entrance of the ice-cream parlor. She had just opened the door when one of the waiters stopped her.

"Sorry, ma'am, but you can't bring that dog in here," he said politely.

Miss Maggie drew herself up to her full height. "Young man, I am here by invitation, and where I go, Ludwig goes. Stand aside!"

The waiter did. Miss Maggie and Ludwig made their way to the Taylors' table, and Doc held her chair as Miss Maggie sat down.

"Here's the *real* hero of the day," Doc said, smiling down at her. "Now the celebration can begin!"

Toby waved at the waiter. "One more banana split, Bob," he said.

Miss Maggie looked down and patted Ludwig. "Make that two!"

Laughing, Val said, "You better order three, Toby. I think Pedro deserves a banana split, too."